BLOWIN' UP A MURDER

KENNI LOWRY MYSTERY

BOOK EIGHT

TONYA KAPPES

TONYA KAPPES
WEEKLY NEWSLETTER

Want a behind-the-scenes journey of me as a writer?
The ups and downs, new deals, book sales, giveaways and more? I share it all! Join the exclusive Southern Sleuths private group today! Go to www.patreon.com/Tonyakappesbooks

As a special thank you for joining, you'll get an exclusive copy of my cross-over short story, *A CHARMING BLEND.* Go to Tonyakappes.com and click on subscribe at the top of the home page.

PREVIEW

The weather outside made the old barn rattle, and the chandelier in the back shake.

We all turned to watched the storm that'd finally rolled over top of the event. The curtains swept up, and the rain pelted through the open door.

Tibbie hurried to the back to pull the two barn doors shut.

Just as she tugged one last time to get the crack between them shut, a bolt of lightning flashed, illuminating the concrete party patio just outside the barn doors.

Shrill shrieks pierced the air inside the barn as the reality of the situation became clear. The spotlight shone on the body lying on the ground.

The waiter.

An umbrella sticking out of his chest.

"It sure has blown up a murder." A slight breeze carried the words to my ear of a voice I knew belonged to my poppa, Tug Lowry.

Who was also dead.

CHAPTER ONE

Oh Finn.

My heart twirled around just looking at him in the suit and out of his Clay's Ferry uniform. I'd seen him in that uniform a lot more often than regular clothes.

I never thought it was going to be a shock to see him in the new navy sheriff's getup since I was used to seeing him in the baby-poop-brown-almost-yellow sheriff's uniform we wore in Cottonwood.

We being me, Scott Lee, and Betty Murphy. I lump Betty in there only because she didn't participate in the uniform daily. She claimed the button-up shirt and pants were too stiff for her arthritis. I would've believed her if she'd worn some sort of easier outfit instead of jeans and a different buttoned cardigan every day. But who was keeping score?

It was one of those things Mama stuck in my head—obey your elders. That went for work as well, even if my elder was an employee.

"What?" Finn caught me looking at him. His freshly cut black hair was shorter than normal, which was fine by me because his big brown eyes became his best feature. His hand held mine, and both of them were resting on his thigh.

"You look handsome." I smiled since this was, like, the umpteenth time I'd told him since he picked me up for the wedding.

A wedding of two people I didn't know and had no clue who these people were. It was one of those invitations where all the government officials were invited, and since all was right in Cottonwood, Scott was at the department in case any calls came in. Scott got the job since it was Saturday and Betty did not work the weekends. I got all gussied up and dragged Finn with me.

He was sort of a buffer between me and Mama, who, by the way, was sitting next to me, sticking her long fingernail into my ribs and giving it a little twist.

"Aren't spring weddings so lovely?" Mama's nail dug a smidgen deeper.

"Stop," I warned with a head jerk her way.

"What?" Mama's Southern drawl came out as if she didn't know what she was doing. "I was talking to Lulu."

"You always have to worry about rain, and from what Edna Easterly posted into today's *Cottonwood Chronicles,* it's gonna come a gusher later on this afternoon." Lulu McClain's head was stuck up between me and Mama's shoulders. She had been seated behind us and scooted up to the edge of the bench, where she laid her forearms along the back of our pew so she and Mama could talk about wedding.

Lulu had short black hair and owned Lulu's Boutique, located on Main Street in downtown Cottonwood. She had very trendy items in the shop that catered to the South, horses, and the state of Kentucky.

By talk, I meant gossip, and they sure didn't care who heard them.

"That's why I think you need to have a summer wedding." Ruby Smith sat by Lulu and put her two cents' worth in, along with light touch on my shoulder. Her short red hairstyle was a staple for Ruby, as was her bright-orange lipstick. She, along with Mama and a few of their other friends in Cottonwood, were known as the Henny Hens, though really most of them were part of the Auxiliary Women's Club, where they'd met years ago.

"Tell her, Viv," Ruby followed up.

She encouraged my mama to keep playing the fantasy in her head that somehow Finn had popped the question, and he had not. He hadn't even mentioned the possibility of us getting married. Though his parents had come to Cottonwood to meet me and my family, and that didn't go over so well.

"Flowers are lovely in the summer. Myra was telling me the other day, when I went down to Petal Pushers to get a spring wreath for the front door, how peonies scream summer wedding with the billowing petals that give off a delightful scent." Mama's excitement was oozing out of her with the thought. "Did you know peonies come in several vibrant pink, yellow, and white hues that would go with any color of bridesmaid's dresses? Plus they are a larger bloom, so you really get more bang for your buck. That's what Myrna said."

"I can see it now." Ruby fanned her jewel-bedecked fingers out in front of her between us. Her arms were filled with bangles that were rattling with the hand swoops. "Gorgeous sunny day with those light pinks on each table in a round glass bowl filled just a little over half with water."

The Henny Hens didn't care what I had to say. They had Mama's back and agreed with her that I was getting older.

If I knew anything about hens, it was they were nosy. Mama and all her friends put their noses in everything. That included everything that was nothing about them. That did make my job a little harder at times, especially when it came to crimes in and around Cottonwood.

They'd hear something on the police scanner—every household had one—and be at the scene before I could get there. Since I was Mama's daughter, they felt they could not only get private police information from me but also tell me how to run the investigation.

"I think fall is lovely too." Mama's chin lifted as she kept her gaze forward before she shifted her eyes enough to take a gander at me and see if I was looking at her.

"And it would give us a few months to prepare." Lulu only made the situation worse.

"Mmmhmm," Mama sighed and looked ahead like I was engaged. "The church is so pretty in the fall too. Myrna did mention how rich and warm fall's most popular blooms can be." Mama gave a very satisfying sigh. "What she said made real sense too." Mama nodded. "She said no matter what the theme of the wedding—like rustic, chic, or classic—all those dramatic orange, red, yellow, purple, and even brown hues found in the fall are gorgeous."

"I'm thinking dahlias." Lulu patted my back. I didn't turn to look at her. "Don't you love the weather in the fall, Kenni?"

"I thought Finn was Cath-o-lick?" Ruby asked, as if the religion left a bad taste in her mouth.

"Do you ladies not see me sitting right here?" Finn dropped my hand and extended his arm over me and rested it around my shoulder, taking up the back of the pew and forcing Ruby and Lulu to scoot back into their seats.

"We are just talkin', Finn. You don't have to act all highfalutin now that you've got that big job in Clay's Ferry." Ruby's remarks to him garnered a few snickers.

"Myrna has done a real fine job with these arrangements, but everyone seems to get married in the spring. Only special weddings are in the fall." Mama had it set in her mind I was getting married in the fall.

Again I shot Mama a look.

"What, Kenni?" Mama put her hand on her chest like she was appalled at me even looking at her. "I didn't say it. Ruby did." She shimmied her shoulders.

The whole religion thing had been a sore topic of conversation, and one Finn and I had both skirted since our parents had had a huge disagreement over which church their grandchildren would attend. *Talk about putting the cart before the horse.*

Finn and I were nowhere near getting married, much less having children.

"Thank you," I whispered to Finn and looked over where I heard the side door in the front of the church open.

A man who I assumed was the groom walked out behind Preacher Bing and four other groomsmen. They had on long black tuxedos with tails and top hats.

"My oh my, they've gone all out." Mama leaned over and acted as if she only wanted me to hear, but the Henny Hens behind her moaned an "Mmhhmmm."

The traditional wedding song filtered over the speakers, signaling us to stand—a tradition we did as soon as the bride appeared to start her walk down the aisle.

I kept facing forward so I didn't have to fight to see the tip-top of the bride's veil over the crowd of people behind me. But the murmurs and gasps along with the clicks of cameras told me she was a sight to behold.

"Kenni."

I heard my name in a faint whisper. Behind Finn's shoulder was Polly Parker Ryland, the first lady of Cottonwood.

"Do you mind moving your head?" She jutted her phone at me, clearly wanting to get a shot of the bride.

I slumped down.

"Those are the family pearls. Antiques." Ruby had leaned forward and wiggled a finger at the bride when she walked past.

Ruby would know what was antique and what wasn't because she owned Ruby's Antiques on Main Street. Treasures to her, but whenever I went in there, it smelled old. That was what antiques were to me. Old.

"Are they?" Mama danced back and forth on her shoes to see around the people in front of us so she could try to get a glimpse of this family heirloom. "She's got too much lace on her face." I could leave it to Mama to find something wrong with the bride. Luckily, she did whisper that, so no one else heard.

Why did weddings always bring out the soft side of people? The entire ceremony, Finn held my hand, squeezing it during the sweet moments that didn't go unnoticed between the bride and groom. They had all the attention on them.

Not mine. I had assessed the church, locating the accessible exits, since some were blocked by candelabras filled to overflowing with wildflowers.

I'd been to church here a million times and knew the exits. It was by habit that I took in all the surroundings for the just-in-case-there's-an-emergency situation. While I did so, I couldn't help but notice one of the groomsmen stood a little further away than the rest and wasn't really included in the heckling some of them gave the groom, to which the bride was all smiles.

The groomsman who was all business had to have been a relative of the groom. After all, he was the one who had the rings in his pocket and seemed to give the groom more sincere, brotherly-love type of interactions during the ceremony.

After the bride and groom kissed and the final trumpet sent them down the aisle, Mama jumped to her feet.

"We've got to go to the reception. I heard it was to die for." Mama would have ridden on the bride's train if she could.

"You've got to wait until they release the pews one by one, Mama." I had to hold her back by keeping a fistful of the back of her dress in hand.

"Now, Kenni, don't be ridiculous. I know what good manners are, but I'm telling you, you might have to use the siren to bypass all the people going to this reception." She loved to think she was always within the law, but when it came time to use me for her good, she was willing to break it.

I gave her another look.

"I know you can't, but it sure would be nice if we got there and got a good seat. You never know." She plucked the white gloves out of her handbag and smacked me with them before she slipped them on her hands. "You might get some good pointers."

"Tibbie has already saved us a seat." I pointed at Mama, me, Finn, and the Henny Hens, which now included Viola White and Myrna Savage, all perched in the row behind us.

Tibbie Bell was one of my best friends, and she was an event planner. When she got the call about this job, we'd heard about it for over a year. Now the big day was here, and honestly I wasn't there with the hopes that the bride and groom would vote for me in the next election, though that was a real reason to come to these things around here. I was there to support Tibbie.

That was the way it was in Cottonwood.

Weddings were as big as having a baby. Having a baby was as big as a funeral. Funerals, well, those were social gatherings not to be missed, no matter how well you knew the deceased.

In Cottonwood those three events were always happening, which meant we were always together and pitched in whenever we could.

When I looked around while waiting for our turn to be let out of the pew, I saw a lot of the townsfolk there with big smiles on their faces, talking to one another, and being neighborly. As the sheriff, I loved seeing the community like that.

Cottonwood wasn't always rosy. I saw a few neighbors here socializing, but if I went to their houses, they'd be bickering back and forth about rose bushes a little over the property line or how someone let their paper sit in their driveway too long.

Not today. Today was a celebration of happiness and love.

"Here you go." The serious groomsman just so happened to be the one who let us out of the pew. "The bride is very environmentally friendly, so they're using bubbles to blow instead of rice to throw." He handed me a clear plastic bottle with bubble water in it.

"Isn't that clever?" Mama looked over her shoulder at me, tipped her chin down, and lifted her brows. "See? Something you can do."

"Keep walking," I told her.

The sunshine filtered through the doors at the back of the church that were spread wide open for us to gather outside.

"Looky there. Clouds." Lulu pointed off to the west where there were a few dark clouds in the sky. "Sunny one minute. Raining the next. That's the spring weather for you."

By the looks of the moving clouds, the rain was going to be coming rather fast.

"I sure hope they make it to the reception before then," Finn said and gestured to a white horse-drawn carriage that was open to the elements.

"Smile, you two love birds!" Edna Easterly held her camera up to her eyes.

I was a little taken aback at Edna's appearance. She wasn't dressed in her fishing vest with all the pockets that held all her journalist gadgets and her feathered fedora hat with the glued-on note card where she'd proudly written Reporter with a marker.

"A little closer, like you are in love." She gestured at us to get a little closer. "Look into the camera and smile!"

As soon as she clicked the shutter, a big bolt of lightning broke through the sky.

"That made me shiver." I shook a bit before the goose bumps crawled along my arms.

"Hmmm." Mama pinched me. "Someone's walking over your grave, Kenni."

CHAPTER TWO

I'd never bring to light what I was thinking after Mama said that to me. It was never good to hear someone tell you someone was walking over your grave. It was like a "bless your heart," only it wasn't the good kind of "bless your heart."

Mama didn't have to tell me anything that I wasn't already feeling. As sheriff, you get keen on your senses, and when something was off, then something was wrong.

Instead of dwelling on that weird and unusual feeling, I chalked it up to the weather and how I felt bad for the bride and groom having to hurry off in the carriage just to make it to the reception. It was being held out at the Cottonwood Barn and Farm, an old barn located in the country in Cottonwood, and probably the only place big enough to accommodate so many guests. Because of its size, it'd been turned into a much-needed events center.

"Isn't it great?" Tibbie bounced with glee. She took in the barn with wide eyes like she'd just seen it for the first time.

Far from it. Tibbie had been talking about this events center for months and tried to get us out here to look at it. I held off after she'd told our group of gal pals about how this was the first wedding in the redone barn.

That was a big deal for her and her business.

"It's beautiful," I agreed, taking in the surroundings. "You know Mama is going to go crazy."

"I know. She'd already pulled me aside to ask about some of the service." Tibbie grinned and jerked up when one of the staff members of the venue called for her. "Don't forget to try the food! This is the first time I've used the caterer, and Venetta's been great!"

I'd noticed the name of the caterer earlier and grinned at the catchy title, That's A Toast.

Though it appeared Tibbie initially had planned for the supper portion of the reception to take place outside, it was nice how there was space indoors to easily move it.

There was a rustic, vintage feel that seemed to fit the couples and their guests. It would be hard not to fall in love with the charming, tranquil countryside that lay just outside of the barn.

"There's even guest houses on the property." Mama had found me. "Kenni," she gasped. "This would be perfect for out-of-town family."

"Who lives out of town?" I asked and grabbed a flute of champagne off the tray of the waiter passing by.

"You mean you wouldn't invite Finn's family?" She asked it like it was a good idea.

"Mama." I lifted the flute to my lips and took a nice swig before I said my piece. I lifted my hand in the air. "There's no ring on this finger. There's no plans for there to be a ring on this finger, so let's just drop it."

"You're right. There might be a better place to host a wedding reception by then." She pinched me, and in an instant she flipped a switch by wearing a huge open-mouthed smile and a wave. "Hi, Darlene!"

She didn't bother telling me goodbye as she darted off to talk to someone she recognized.

The back of the barn had the double doors open to take in the scenery. By the way the gray clouds were rolling in, I was sure it was already raining in downtown Cottonwood.

The sheer curtains hanging over the door and down each side waved a little as the breeze from the oncoming storm brushed past. The pink chandelier, dead center of the door and dangling from one of the cedar beams above, swayed some before the crystals made a light clinking noise.

On each side of the door were old bourbon barrels with boxes for cash presents, along with some cute signs that read Mr. and Mrs., and on the floor next to them were two umbrella stands with the bride and groom's names on them.

Nice touch, Tibbie, I thought.

Cheers filtered through the opposite end of the barn. I turned around. The groomsmen and bridesmaids were walking inside. Several of the bridesmaids had their bouquets raised above their heads, swirling them around in celebration of what the night was going to bring.

The DJ was playing Garth Brooks's "Friends in Low Places," which I found a little odd for a wedding since the song was about an ex showing up at the bride's wedding.

The best man was singing it so loud, he grabbed a shot glass off of the waiter's tray and raised it high in the air before he downed it.

The waiter shook his head and kept walking.

They'd be partying it up while I'd be long asleep. Not that I was old and didn't love a good time—very much the opposite—but I had to work a full shift in the morning, and there was nothing worse than sitting at my desk in the department.

The sheriff's department was located in the back of Cowboy's Catfish Restaurant, and smelling fried fish while nursing a hangover didn't mix with my stomach.

The song got cut off, and the DJ started another, much more appropriate, song.

I couldn't stop smiling when the DJ played a song and announced the names of the wedding party before he did the grand introduction of the bride and groom.

"Join me in welcoming Mr. and Mrs. Dickie Dee!" The DJ barely got it out as the guests erupted in cheers and woot woots.

My champagne glass was still full, so I gave a half-hearted clap then downed the rest of the flute before I set it down on one of the empty tray stations next to me.

Finn's eyes caught mine. He was leaving the hors d'oeuvres stand with a plate piled high. I lifted my chin with a smile to welcome him.

"These people went all out," Finn said and held up the snacks after he'd made it over to me.

"They did. I can't wait to see what kind of business Tibbie gets from this." Saying her name, I looked for her to check in to see what she was doing.

Over the crowd, I spotted the messy yet fashionable bun her long brown hair had been professionally styled in in a different part of the barn where there were very long tables and chairs.

The tables went along with the rustic feel, as they were made out of reclaimed barnwood. She'd kept the romantic feel by putting lacy runners down the middle of each table with lots of greenery, soft pink and cream roses, and gold-speckled candleholders nestled every few inches with a glowing candle inside.

Each seat had a place setting with a gold charger that held a cream plate with gold edging. Even the neatly and correctly placed silverware was far from silver. It was gold.

"Who are these people?" I asked Finn and took one of the cheese crackers off his plate. "Mmhhh." There was no denying this fancy cheese. "This is a long way from our spray cheese," I joked.

"No kidding. Maybe I can sneak some of these in my suit pocket." He wiggled his brows.

"Good idea." I took another one and laughed before I popped it into my mouth. I nudged him and gestured to the serious groomsman.

"What about him?" Finn asked.

"I wonder if he's the brother of the groom. He seems to want everything to go smooth." I noticed him looking at the table setting, moving a few things and showing Tibbie something.

Her messy bun flung up and down as she nodded her head in agreement to whatever he was saying.

"Excuse me for a minute," I told Finn when I saw Tibbie start from the top of one dinner table and rearrange a few things. "I'm going to help Tibbie."

"I'll go talk to Luke." Finn took his plate and walked over to some of the guests we did know.

The groomsman had passed by me and stopped where a few of the other groomsmen were throwing back a few shots of something.

"How are you doing with all this?" I heard one of them ask the serious groomsman.

"He got the sloppy seconds." His words seemed a bit off.

Sloppy seconds. I rolled my eyes so hard I saw my brain. What a jerk, I thought. Since he was a big baby, his ego had gotten bruised from whatever history the other guys were referring to.

"What can I do?" I asked Tibbie.

"Apparently, I put the salad fork and the shrimp fork in the wrong place." She looked relieved when I walked up. "Do you mind?"

"Nope. I'd love to help." I walked over to the other side of the table. "You do that side, and I'll do this side."

"I'll be so glad when this is over and tonight we will enjoy a late-night euchre game." Tibbie had organized a late-night game, and since we were all at the wedding, she thought we might as well continue the night with our weekly game.

We'd gotten the first table rearranged then started on the second one.

"Have you ever seen such?" Tibbie whispered over the table and held up the gold fork.

"Gold silverware?" I laughed at the oxymoron. "Is it real?"

"Oh," she scoffed. "Yes. This is old money. Kentucky old money. See that person over there?"

I glanced over my shoulder.

"Edna?" I asked. I thought Tibbie was referring to Edna Easterly, who was taking so many photos. Initially I thought the bride and groom had hired her for the wedding, but now that I saw the videographer and what appeared to be a real wedding photographer, I knew Edna was here to get photos for the society section of the *Cottonwood Chronicles*.

"No!" Tibbie chuckled. "The real people. Those people are from *Barnwood Brides*. That big magazine. If this wedding goes exactly like I planned it, they are going to do a spread in their magazine, and my name, my business, will go in."

She curled her lips in as if she didn't want to squeal out loud, letting her eyes bulge as if the excitement inside needed to find a place.

"Tibbie!" I was so excited for her. "That's amazing news."

"And all those girls up front there" —she pointed to the bridesmaids —"they are all engaged and took my card. Now you see why I've been talking about this event for so long."

"I know you're going to be so popular from this. Amazing." I was so proud of my friend.

The DJ had turned off the song as the string orchestra took over.

My eyes grew wide, and I slid them over the table at Tibbie in disbelief.

"They spared no expense for their daughter." She threw a sweet smile on when the mother of the bride walked past.

I recognized her from the wedding.

"Everything is looking lovely," she complimented Tibbie. "I can tell the magazine is very interested."

"I'm so glad. It's your gorgeous daughter who is the centerpiece." Tibbie was so good at brownnosing her clients.

Both of us hurried to get the gold forks properly placed, since the next thing on the program was the toast and the invite for everyone to take their seat.

Finn and I sat at a table in the far back along with the other government employees, which included Mayor Chance Ryland and his wife, Polly Parker Ryland.

"Have you ever seen the like, Kenni?" Polly Parker was in her element. She picked up the gold fork. "I was just telling Chance I've been looking at gold silverware for our home." Her perfectly lined pink pouty mouth contorted with envy, her nose curled as she looked at me. "Ain't that right, honey?"

"Mmhmm, dear." That was Mayor Ryland's standard answer.

"If she thinks he can afford that on his mayor salary, she's more distorted than that marriage of hers," Vita Jones said under her breath, nearly making me choke on my spit.

Vita was a hoot and a half. She was married to Luke Jones, who sat on the town council.

As soon as the toasts began, the thunder and lightning started outside.

The lights inside the venue were brought down to a glow and a spotlight placed on the bridal party table.

One by one the bridesmaids gave a sweet toast about the bride and how she was such a great friend. The spotlight followed each speaker.

Of course the groomsmen were much different. They gave the groom more of a roasting about his raucous past that included a few women along the way.

"Bradley!" The DJ called over the speaker when it was the best man's turn. The spotlight was focused on Bradley's empty seat.

The groomsmen started to smack the top of their table, chanting Bradley's name.

The weather outside made the old barn rattle, and the chandelier in the back shake.

We all turned to watched the storm that'd finally rolled over top of the event. The curtains swept up, and the rain pelted through the open door.

Tibbie hurried to the back to pull the two barn doors shut.

Just as she tugged one last time to get the crack between them shut, a bolt of lightning flashed, illuminating the concrete party patio just outside the barn doors.

Shrill shrieks pierced the air inside the barn as the reality of the situation became clear. The spotlight shone on the body lying on the ground.

The waiter.

An umbrella sticking out of his chest.

"It sure has blown up a murder." A slight breeze carried the words to my ear of a voice I knew belonged to my poppa, Tug. Who was dead.

CHAPTER THREE

"Excuse me, excuse me." I had gone up to grab the microphone from the DJ. "I'm Sheriff Kendrick Lowry. I'm going to need everyone to stay put."

Scott Lee hurried up to the DJ booth.

"Deputy, I need you to secure the barn and have anyone who might have been handling this reception and all the guests detained." I had barely finished my sentence before Scott hurried off with Tibbie Bell in his sights.

"What can I do?" Finn asked, even though he already knew what needed to happen.

"You can take yourself right on over to your table since you got fired." Poppa had appeared right up next to Finn.

I shifted my eyes slightly past Finn's shoulder so I could give Poppa the eye. I didn't need him whispering things that did not pertain to the issue at hand.

Murder.

I glanced around the room. Everyone was in shock as they were all trying to figure out exactly what was going on.

Max Bogus, the county coroner, was sitting at a table with Mayor Ryland, Polly, and the Joneses.

"Max Bogus." I gave him a nod, grateful everyone who needed to be here at the crime scene was already here. "Please and thank you very much."

Good manners never did go out of style, and even though this was a grave situation, it was still better to be polite.

He ran his napkin across his lips as he jumped up, knocking over a few water glasses as his thighs hit the edge of the table, causing Polly Parker Ryland to jump to her feet, only to take a tumble when her heels gave out.

"Polly!" Mayor Ryland was quick to his feet to help her up.

"Listen here." The bride ran over, all that crinoline on her fancy wedding dress crumpled up in the crook of her arm, her bouquet flailing around in front of her as she wagged it in my face. "I don't know what is going on here."

I pushed the bouquet away.

"This is my day. I don't know who that is, but it has to be moved. I'm not going to stand here and let you—" Her eyes searched around for something on me, maybe my badge.

"Sheriff Kendrick Lowry," I informed her.

"That body has to be moved." She let go of the dress and snapped her finger at the DJ. "Music! Now!"

"No." My head swiveled on my shoulders and I gave a stern warning to the DJ. "Don't you dare turn that music on. This is a crime scene, and we are going to need everyone to cooperate."

"No!" The bride got right back up into my face. "My guests are going to finish eating their supper, then we are going to dance and have cake, and I'm going on my honeymoon."

"I'm sorry, but that's not going to happen." I had to be straight with her.

"Daddy! Daddy!" she screamed, and before I could do anything, she whacked me over the head with the bouquet. "You are going to leave right now!"

"I guess that's one way to get the bouquet so you can get that daughter of yours hitched," I heard Viola White say.

"You are going to be put under arrest for assaulting a police officer if you don't stop!" I had my hands over my head to try to stop her from hitting me. "Is this how you want to spend your honeymoon night?"

"Do something, Daddy! You made me invite all of these government people, and now they are ruining my wedding." She whacked with every word.

It seemed like a long time, but in reality, it wasn't but about forty-five seconds before Finn had grabbed her around the waist and picked her up. But the flailing continued with all four limbs moving in a bicycle motion.

"Get. Your. Hands. Off. Me!" The bride's voice got angrier and louder the further away she got from me, as Finn carefully backed up with her flailing around like a fish out of water in his arms.

"I'm sorry about this." I put the microphone back up to my mouth and looked past everyone to the back where the body was lying. Max had used one of the white tablecloths to put over the deceased. "Tibbie, if you don't mind bringing up the lights."

The lights were still on low beam for the romantic ambiance, and there was not one bit of low light that was going to even give a hint of that emotion at this current time.

"I'm going to need everyone to stay at their table." I looked behind me when there was a bit of rustling at the wedding party table. Bradley, the groomsman, was shuffling behind all the chairs.

He had his palm tight against the black tuxedo jacket so it didn't hit anyone's head as he moved behind them to get to his seat.

"You might as well get comfortable, because this is going to take a while to take everyone's statements."

Finn had to take the bride out of the barn in order for her to stop throwing her hissy fit.

I put down the microphone and unplugged the DJ's cords in case the bride came back and decided to spin the tunes herself. I had to give it to her—a dead body didn't seem to bother her one bit, which was odd.

"I'll start with the wedding party," I told Scott after I'd finally made it over to him and the body. Max Bogus was doing his best to assess what had happened, even though we could clearly see the man had been stabbed with an umbrella.

Not just any umbrella.

The wedding umbrella.

Scott shook his head, and we went opposite ways. He took the table closest to the back of the barn where the party patio was located. If anyone had seen something, it had to be them.

"Hi there." My Southern accent filled the silence of the wedding party. Quiet whispers fluttered behind me. I started my introduction. "I'm Sheriff—"

"We know who you are. You ruined Jasmine and Dickie's wedding." Bradley snickered from his seat next to the groom.

The groom nudged him to hush.

Bradley covered his mouth with his hand, hiding his laughter.

"That one there is one to look out for." Poppa ghosted himself behind Bradley. "He's wet too. No umbrella."

"It's my understanding everyone in the bridal party got an umbrella with the happy couple's monogram." I smiled sweetly at the group. "Bradley, is it?"

The grin that had been on his face faded to a stern, sinister look.

"I recall that during the toast and before our friend was found dead, an umbrella stuck through his chest"—out of the corner of my eye I could see the sheer horror on the others' faces—"that you were missing. Didn't y'all here start to chant and even bang on the table?"

Slowly I slid my eyes down the table of the wedding party and made sure to make eye contact. Bradley was the only one who didn't have a look of fear on his face.

"I oughta wipe that smirk off of him right now, Kenni bug." Poppa never liked anyone to disrespect a person of the law, especially when it came to me. "Let me just do a little something like rattle his chair leg. That'll straighten him up."

As much as I'd have loved to see some fright put into Bradley's face, there was no time for ghost shenanigans.

I gave a slow shake to my head.

"You're no fun. Use me. Let me shake up this jerk." Poppa had not been like this when he was sheriff of Cottonwood, Kentucky. He was always by the book, but now that he was a ghost deputy, which was still hard for me to even swallow, he liked to use his invisibility to anyone but me and Duke, my dog, to my advantage, so we could get crimes solved.

This would be the eighth time I'd seen the ghost of my poppa, and that meant eight crimes.

I thought I was a true badass when it came to zero crime when I took over as sheriff of our small town, but in reality it was the ghost of my poppa who was scaring off any crime so I was safe.

Unfortunately even a ghost can't be in two places at once. When there was a murder and a break-in a few years ago, well, that's when I discovered I'd had a ghost deputy and didn't know it.

Too bad he only showed up when there was a crime, because I sure did miss him a lot. Another thing, I couldn't even really talk to him when he was here, or people would think I was crazy talking to myself.

The embarrassment I caused my mama today would be nothing compared to what rumors of me talking to myself would do to her. It'd send her straight to the loony bin.

"And by the look of your tuxedo jacket, it looks like you were out in the rain without the umbrella the bride and groom I'm sure paid a pretty penny for." The smirk faded from his face. He drummed his fingers along the top of the table. "Is there something you'd like to tell me?"

"Nope." He lifted those drumming fingers up, giving me a hand gesture. "I've got nothing to hide. I was outside smoking."

"In the rain?" I asked.

"I vape. It doesn't require a flame." His right brow lifted, a condescending look in his eyes.

"I've never liked a punk. You just need to take him on down to the jail cell and see if that suits him." Poppa had all sorts of illegal activities he wanted me to perform.

"Excuse me, Kenni," A hand touched my arm, and I turned around to find Preacher Bing slightly behind me. "Can I have a word with you?"

My mama's eyes pierced through the crowd and seared right through him.

"Your mama asked me to come over." He smiled and looked back where Mama's scowl had been replaced by her friendly smile.

It was something she did. She could give me the look at a moment's notice, and if someone glanced her way, she'd switch it off in a split second.

"She's wondering if there's any way you can do this differently."

"And just how can I do that? Pick up the dead body and move it to another location where it wasn't found and lose all this evidence?" I pulled back and smiled. "Now Preacher, you aren't asking me for the sake of embarrassing my mama to not find justice for that poor man who is lying underneath a tablecloth. After all, he has a mama, and I'm sure she'd love to see him alive at this moment."

"Yes. I'll go speak to Viv." He tugged his lips together.

"You be sure to put a little more in the collection plate this week too." I winked and sucked in a deep breath before I turned back around to look at Bradley. "I'm sorry about that. Mothers. I'm guessing you have one of those, right, Bradley?"

"Yeah." He snorted like I was an idiot. I didn't like anyone thinking I was an idiot.

"I'm sure she told you never to go outside in the rain because you can catch a cold." It was an old wives' tale, but at this moment he was all I had as a suspect. "I'd love to take you back to the sheriff's department for a friendly chat."

"Do I need a lawyer?" He suddenly seemed a bit anxious.

"Only if you did something wrong," I said, never once taking my eyes off him. Reading his body language was so important, but not looking at Poppa was a priority.

"I did nothing wrong," he insisted.

"Good then. Why don't we take it on down to the station." I knew by the noise behind me that Max Bogus had gotten ahold of someone down at the funeral home to send down a hearse and a church cart so they could take the body.

Reluctantly Bradley stood up and gave the groom a pat on the back, the good-ole-boy-style back smack, while I waited patiently for him to emerge from behind the table.

Not being in a rush had become a skill. Of course when I was just out of the academy and a crime happened, the first thing I wanted to do was jump on it. What I'd come to learn was slow and patient was a surefire way to get the killer or criminal. Wait them out.

I had no problem waiting Bradley out until he talked.

"I'm not going to be able to show my face again," Mama cried loud enough for me to hear as I ushered Bradley past her on our way out the barn door.

CHAPTER FOUR

"Deputy Lee." I started giving orders with the little time I had left. I needed to get a lot accomplished after he'd stuck Bradley in the back of his deputy truck. It wasn't like we could leave the scene just yet.

It was only the two of us in the department, and if either of us left, we'd never get through all the guests to start questioning them.

"I need you to get all the overhead lights pulled up, these floodlights on. "I pointed to the lights on the outside of the barn when I noticed they were there. "These low-hanging clouds don't look like they're moving anytime soon."

I wasn't going to complain about how the rain had slowed to a spit. It wasn't like it was night—it was not. It was an afternoon wedding, but the day was filled with gray, almost black clouds that hung so low it made it feel like night.

"Kenni! Kenni!" Mama stood at the door, wagging one of the wedding umbrellas in the air. "Honey, you need to cover up. You might catch a cold!"

"I'm fine, Mama," I assured her. Scott laughed. "Nothing like an investigation with Mama around."

"You're lucky you've got a mama who cares." The tone in Scott's voice plucked a chord within me, making me wonder exactly what he'd meant. He headed back inside.

It wasn't like we knew each other all that well. When he came to work at the department, we'd pretty much kept it professional.

"Yoo-hoo! Kenni!" Mama yelled.

"Mama, I said I was fine. I'll be in soon," I assured her right before the floodlight clicked on. "You do me a big favor and don't you dare let anyone leave that barn!"

Mama's eyes grew real big. With confidence she gave a big nod, pinched her lips, and took the order very serious.

"That should give her something to do." I looked down at the concrete for any visible evidence. The waiter was wet, so he had to have been outside.

There were a few muddy footprints around the outdoor cigarette deposit stand next to the door.

"Don't let anyone out here," I told Scott when he came back outside. "I've got to go get my bag."

I slipped my heels off, not only because I could walk faster from here to the parking lot where Finn had parked the old Wagoneer, but the spikes on my shoes were sinking into the wet grass.

I could've taken the walkway to the parking lot, but my Jeep was clear to the other side, and it was faster to cut through the grass.

"What do you think we've got, Kenni bug?" Poppa's ghost was sitting in the back seat as if he were waiting for me.

"A dead body, an umbrella, and a cold, rainy afternoon." I looked at him and opened up the duffle bag I kept in the car with an extra set of clothes and shoes.

"Did you see anything?" I asked him as I unzipped the bag to get out the pair of tennis shoes before I wiggled my feet into the tied shoes and stomped them on the ground to get the heel of the shoes on.

"Too early to tell, but look around, very carefully. There's something out there. Some sort of clues. Everyone is a suspect." He didn't have any words of wisdom but the ones I already knew. "This is very early in the investigation. See what Max has to say and then go from there."

"I don't have to wait for Max to tell me this was a murder." The umbrella did that.

"Just like I said." Poppa's ghost started to evaporate. "Photos, videos, revenge."

"Revenge?" I asked just as he whispered away. "Where are you going? I need you. Aren't you my ghost deputy?"

"Ghost deputy?" Finn laughed. "You mean as in a ghost writer? I help you, but no one knows since we aren't on the same team anymore?"

"Yep." I turned around. "That's right. I need your help while you're here."

I turned back around and closed my eyes really hard, remembering just how careful I had to be when I talked to Poppa. People seeing me talking to Poppa, even if it was Finn, made me look crazy. I looked like I was talking to myself.

"Here." I grabbed a few of the evidence markers from the floor-board. "We need to make sure no one leaves until we get their name and phone numbers and see if they will either let us download their photos right now or send them to me."

"Sounds good." Finn's face changed from the loving boyfriend to the serious sheriff. "I'm more than happy to be your ghost deputy."

He took off while I leaned into the car a little further to grab my bag where I kept all the things necessary for a crime scene.

"I'd say, "Over my dead body will that boy take my job,' but I'm dead." Poppa reappeared.

"At least he didn't run off." I had to let my poppa know I didn't like him ghosting in and out without telling me what he was doing. "Where did you go?"

"I counted eleven umbrellas and twelve wedding party members. At first I wondered if some guests had gotten an umbrella as a souvenir, but now that I've done a little further investigating, I do believe they were only bought for the wedding party." Poppa looked up to the barn. "It was his seat that was missing the umbrella."

I looked back at Scott's truck. Bradley was watching me.

"Yeah. He knows more than he's saying." I tried to talk with my mouth closed so Bradley didn't see.

When I walked back to the barn, I had a tight grip on my bag and didn't dare look Bradley's way, though I could feel the burn of his stare.

I set my bag on top of the concrete on the party patio and unzipped it.

"Is there anything I can do?" a woman in her midfifties asked. Her shirt had her name embroidered on it.

Venetta.

"Venetta, are you in charge of catering?" I asked.

"I'm the owner of the company. I come to all the events." Her being here made it much easier for me than trying to track her down.

"Then I do need to talk to you." I took out two pairs of surgical booties and two pairs of gloves. I gave a set of gloves and booties to Scott. "Here."

Finn had already placed a couple of the evidence markers around the footprints and taken the camera out of my bag to snap a few photos.

"Anything you need." She gasped when Max Bogus passed by us, the church cart rattling with the weight of the body underneath an appropriate corpse cloth.

I slid Scott a look, and he sidled up to Venetta, taking her by the arm. He walked her over to one of the wrought-iron chairs and swept his hand across the seat to get the puddled water off.

"Kenni." Max Bogus stopped shy of me.

"Anything?" I asked in hopes there'd be some evidence on the body.

"I'm not so sure until I get some X-rays." That was a new one. Max had generally given me a few possible options.

"Kenni bug." Poppa stood next to the body. "I think the umbrella was shoved into him postmortem."

I gulped, trying not to even flinch. If that was this case, the murderer was someone very angry. A hate crime, if you will.

"Don't cut him open until you get the X-rays." I told him. "I want to make sure what his insides say before you break open his chest cavity."

"That's right, Kenni bug. Let the body tell you what happened." Poppa disappeared.

CHAPTER FIVE

The old Wagoneer rattled to life after I let Bradley sit in the passenger seat and got the key into the ignition.

"I hope you don't mind dog hair." I could see the look on his face when he noticed Duke's hair was all over his black tuxedo jacket. "My deputy dog, Duke, rides shotgun."

"When I'm not here." Poppa appeared right in between me and Bradley with his body sitting on the edge of the bench seat in the back.

"What?" I asked Bradley. "Cat got your tongue? You were all willing to talk back at the reception."

I wanted to make sure he knew the sudden shift in his behavior had not gone unnoticed.

"I guess I'm not up to talking until my lawyer is present." Bradley played the lawyer card, which was fine with me.

"Alright then. I'll have Betty call your lawyer when we get to the department." I flipped on the radio to some pop music and tapped the wheel to the beat.

The radio screeched and squalled as Poppa switched the station.

"My car," Poppa proudly stated.

"What the?" Bradley jerked back, pushing up against the seat as far back away from the radio as he could get himself.

"What?" I played dumb, though it was a little enjoyable to see the man frightened.

"The radio just turned itself." He stuttered the words out.

"For heaven's sake, Bradley." I pished it. "This is an old Wagoneer, and things just happen. Sometimes the windows roll down on their own too." I flipped the windshield wipers on high.

The wind had whipped up, and the rain was coming down sideways.

About that time Poppa put his arm between the passenger seat and the door, slowly cranking the window down.

Bradley jerked to his left, pushing away from the door.

"Are you alright, Bradley?" I asked as if nothing were wrong. "You seem pretty jumpy. Maybe you should stop smoking those vape things. Can't be good for your health."

I let go of a long sigh and kept silent as we headed toward Main Street, which was just about fifteen minutes from the barn, so the drive wasn't too painful. Bradley didn't make a peep.

When we passed Lulu's Boutique on the right on our way into town, the On The Run food truck was parked up to the curb, and Jolee Fischer was in the window serving up something good. The rain didn't look like it kept people away.

My mind strayed from Bradley to Jolee. I wondered why she wasn't at the wedding. Or at least there to help Tibbie. The three of us were thick as thieves, and it never crossed my mind to ask. Instead my mind was too occupied by Mama and all the things her mind was percolating about any sort of wedding ideas she had for me. But I knew Jolee would be at euchre, so I'd ask her then.

My eyes shifted to the cemetery on the left when we passed, then they moved to the rearview, where Poppa still sat in his ghostly form.

"I can see what you're thinkin'." He tapped his thick finger to his temple. "You and me need to have a talk."

He was exactly right. I tried not to smile. After Poppa had died, I found visiting the cemetery to be rather comforting when I became sheriff and had to deal with the everyday hard knocks that came with the job, not only politically but also being a woman sheriff in a mostly male government in Cottonwood.

You can hear Mama now, telling me how it wasn't fittin' for a girl to be sheriff, but it was reputable to have a secretary job for the sheriff. I'd decided to skip all that a long time ago, and it was no different today.

I'd gotten used to disappointing Mama, and at this point in my life, it was almost enjoyable just to see what kind of rise I could get out of her.

Today was going to be the icing on the cupcakes.

She'd be gabbing about this wedding, not to mention the dead body, but the thought of me stopping the reception due to the crime scene and the bride physically assaulting me, well, I was sure I'd get a call from Daddy by the end of the night letting me know Mama had taken to the bed.

I turned the old Wagoneer down the alley where the department was located in the rear of Cowboy's Catfish, a local diner downtown. Now it might seem weird to some folks that the government would lease such a space from inside of a restaurant, and I'd agree if we weren't in Cottonwood. The town was just a blip on the map in the state of Kentucky, and well, there was really no crime to even need a big-time facility.

We had everything we needed. A one-room cell in the corner of the office and three desks—one for me, one for Scott, and one for Betty Murphy. Duke even had his own dog bed there, along with a jar of treats.

The closet was a great place to store any extra uniforms and where the printer was located along with the fax machine. Plus we had our very own food service from the other side of the door whenever we wanted it.

"Where are you taking me?" Bradley looked a little scared after I'd pulled up to the dumpster real tight.

"You'll see," I said and got out of the car to walk around and get him. I noticed Poppa was gone, and figured he'd already gone inside the department.

"I don't think this is right?" Bradley gave a little tug of his shoulders when he turned around to look at me as I kept a grip on his cuffs.

"Oh, it's right, alright." I jerked my hand to push him forward.

"What kind of town is this?" Bradley tried to wiggle. "Crazy people around here. There's a killer on the loose, and I didn't do it. Now you've got me cuffed and going into some back alley."

We stopped at the door. I put the key in and opened the lock, deliberately not saying anything.

"Uh-uh. I'm not going in there. I want my lawyer," he protested, the rain beating down a little heavier now.

With a little forceful coaxing, I got me and him through the door.

"I'm sorry. I rarely do my hair, and today was a special day." I tried to speak to him as kindly as I could. "Was a special day for Jasmine and Dickie Dee until you ruined it and my hair."

I gently guided him toward the cell in the far corner.

"Is this the department you so boldly said you were taking me to?" Bradley had that smirky grin on his face.

"Mmhmmm." Once in the cell, I uncuffed his hands and left, shutting the cell door and locking it behind me.

"Really? Am I on *Punk'd*?" He threw his hands in the air. "I get it. Jasmine and Dickie are getting me back for the bachelor party. Right? The waiter person isn't dead, but since I was outside smoking, they knew it would be a funny joke. Okay, take me back to the reception." His voice was loud, like he was trying to let anyone hear him.

"I thought you said you vaped."

"Smoke, vaped. All the same." He walked over to the bars and curled a hand around one. "Listen, this is a joke, right? Prank?"

"This is no joke." I sat down in my desk chair and took out the paperwork I needed for the crime scene investigation.

The door between Cowboy's Catfish and the department opened, and Bartleby Fry stuck his head around.

"Kenni, I heard what happened, and I figured you didn't get to eat, so I made up some fresh hush puppies and cod for you." He pushed the Styrofoam food container through the door.

"Hilarious!" Bradley smacked his hands together. "This is just like that old show with that crazy deputy and sheriff." He scratched his chin. "I can't think of it, but my granddad used to love it."

"The Andy Griffith Show?" Bradley asked.

"Yep! That! Come on, guys. The joke is on me. You got me." Bradley voice got louder with each word.

"Why are you yelling?" I asked and waved Bartleby to come on in.

"So the recording device can hear me." He snorted. "Where is it?"

"Shoowee, Kenni, you've got you one today." Bartleby's eyes grew. He shook his head and walked out of the department.

"What did that mean?" Bradley pointed to himself. "Is he talking about me or this?" He pointed around the department.

I sucked in a deep breath, about to go through the entire process again in hopes he'd hear me this time, but the door to the outside flung open, the rain rushed in, and so did Betty Murphy.

"I reckon we gonna be working late. I got word on the scanner about the big murder." Betty's voice quivered as she shook off the pellets of rain from her umbrella before she fully came in from the wet and now cold outside. "Oh dear."

Her blue eyes focused on Bradley.

"Goodness gracious. I knew something was going to happen when I saw the big thunder cloud rolling into town." She untied the small string underneath her chin that kept her rain bonnet in place. She tucked it down in her pocketbook in the crook of her arm.

"Are you from the local theater company? Because for your age, you play a good Aunt Bee. Wasn't that her name?" Bradley was digging a deeper and deeper hole.

Betty jerked up and looked at Bradley. I knew she was storing every single detail up in her brain so when she talked to her friends, she'd have all the details right.

Cottonwood wasn't a very big town. With the help of Betty Murphy, Mama, and her Henny Hens, not much remained private. Not even things that happened here in the sheriff's department.

"I heard your mama about died." Betty stopped at my desk on the way to her desk to see what was in the box.

"You can have it," I told her. "I'm not hungry."

"Really?" Bradley sounded exhausted. "Can we just stop the play pretending and get on it?"

"So you do want to give me your statement without your lawyer?" I asked.

"Wait." He hesitated with one hand pushed out in front of him, his fingers spread apart. "Is this for real? Like for real real?"

"What did you think this was?" Betty was old-school when it came to respecting your elders. It was something that was taken very seriously around here, and I could tell by the tone in her voice she'd not approved of how Bradley was treating the situation.

"He thinks this is some sort of prank the bride and groom have played on him." I could tell by his fidgeting the reality of where he was had started to sit in his bones.

His face stilled. His Adam's apple bobbled up and down as his eyes shifted around the room. He picked up the pace as he walked in the cell.

"You want me to call Clay's Ferry to pick him up?" Betty asked. "Just so you know, we are just a holding station for the big house. That's over in Clay's Ferry."

"Big house?" He hurried back to the bars. "This isn't a joke, is it?"

"Did Sheriff Lowry ever tell you it was a joke?" Betty popped one of the hush puppies in her mouth. "You better wise up. If I'm not mistaken, I believe you're about to be arrested for the murder of..."

"Gary Futch." I looked through the notes Scott had taken at the scene for me from the caterer who'd employed Mr. Futch.

He'd also noted his conversation with Venetta Stenner, the owner of That's A Toast, the catering company and Gary Futch's employer. According to Scott's notes, Venetta paid a flat fee of two hundred dollars per catering job, and that's what Gary would be paid at the end of the night. He'd worked a few of her jobs over the past six months. He was always on time, and she'd never had a problem with him. No known disagreements with any other catering events, and she didn't have any idea about his personal life. "Quiet and shy" was how she described him.

Interesting. Someone with such an exemplary work ethic and being shy as well as quiet normally didn't get an umbrella shoved into their body.

"So either you better start talking, or call your lawyer." Betty didn't even look at him when she told him his options. She'd moved on to the coleslaw.

"I want to talk to my lawyer." Bradley's lips buttoned up once again after he'd given Betty his lawyer's information.

"Are you sure? There's no one that's going to be more understanding to your situation than me at this moment." It was time for me to soften a smidgen. If I wanted to get him to talk, I was going to have to use honey and not vinegar. "Things happen."

"I want a cigarette." Bradley eyeballed me. "I need a smoke. Can I get one?"

I gave a slight lift of the chin to Betty. "I'll be right back." I grabbed my badge off the desk. "Keep an eye on him."

I got up and headed to the door between the department and Cowboy's Catfish. It wasn't too long ago when customers could smoke at the bar in the greasy spoon restaurant. There were a few grumbles from Bartleby's regulars, but the food and conversation with friends kept them coming back. Taking smoke breaks outside was fine for them.

"Order up!" Bartleby yelled and put a couple of plates of food in the pass-through window between the restaurant and the kitchen. "Kenni. You okay?"

"I'm good. Who out there smokes?" I stood in the hallway outside the door to Bartleby's kitchen.

Without question, he bent down over the grill and looked out the pass-through into the restaurant.

"Any one of those men out there butted up to the counter." He wagged his spatula at me.

"Thanks." I headed down the hall, my stomach growling. I put my hand on it and decided I did need to eat something. It was going to be a long night.

I headed straight to the barstools and approached the first man.

"Sheriff Kenni Lowry." I flashed my badge.

He pulled back and stared at me from underneath the bill of his cap.

"I need a cigarette, and I understand from Mr. Fry you may have one that I can have." My eyes drew past him to the next few men down the row who were now staring at me. "Please."

"Yeah. Um. Sure." He leaned back on his hip and pulled out a crunched-up pack of cigarettes. Hard box. He handed it to me. "Take it."

"I just need one." I opened it and took one out. "Thank you so much. The town of Cottonwood appreciates your donation."

I smiled and gave a nod to the other gentleman before I headed back to the department.

When I opened the door, Betty had turned her chair to the cell and stared straight ahead at Bartleby.

"She didn't take her eyes off me at all." Bradley snickered and jerked forward, trying to get Betty to flinch. "Nothing. She's like steel."

"Thank you, Betty." I held the cigarette up in the air. "You want this, right?"

"Yes." He put his arm through the bars.

"There's no smoking in public government buildings." I carefully laid the smoke on top of my desk. "But if you answer me a few questions, I'm more than happy to take you outside and let you puff away."

"Nah," he snarled. "I think I'll wait for my lawyer."

Betty held up the piece of paper with the lawyer's name and number on it.

I took the piece of paper from Betty and sat down at my desk. I picked up the phone and dialed the lawyer's number. When he answered, I said, "Good evening, Mr. Pennington. Matt Pennington?"

I moved the receiver from my chin and gave Bradley a smile.

"Good." I noted when he confirmed who he was. "I'm Sheriff Kenni Lowry from Cottonwood, Kentucky, and we've got a client of yours, a

Mr. Bradley Ines, here in custody for questioning related to a murder investigation."

The lawyer mumbled some words.

"Yes. A murder in-vest-igation." I made sure he heard me correctly. "I'm sure he is a good man, but we have reason to hold him, and he's asked for your assistance. We are located behind Cowboy's Catfish in downtown Cottonwood, Kentucky. We will be awaiting your arrival, and according to him, it's going to be a few hours."

Betty grabbed another hush puppy out of the food container and stuffed it in her mouth.

"I'm telling you that you better stop eating like that, Betty." Poppa had appeared over Betty's shoulder. "You're gonna end up like me." He held his chest and pretended to be stumbling backwards. "Ain't that right, Kenni bug?"

"Betty, are you okay?" I asked, taking my poppa's not-so-subtle cue to say something to Betty.

"Mmhmmm." She hummed through a mouthful of the doughy, delicious, fried goodness.

"You can go home if you want. I can miss euchre night and stay here with him until the attorney gets here." I wanted to make sure she knew she didn't have to stay, especially since I knew her bedtime was around eight o'clock.

"Y'all still having euchre, even after the wedding?" She cocked her head and looked up at me.

"You're serious. This isn't a prank, is it?" Bradley's emotions were on a roller coaster.

"This boy thinks the sun comes up just to hear him crow." Poppa stood at the bars of the cell, looking at a very fidgety Bradley. "Let him squirm a while. He'll get the hint."

It was interesting, because I couldn't decide if he was honestly shocked he was here and didn't do it or trying to play a really good part. Generally I was great at reading body language, but Bradley was one of those types who appeared to always be a little shady, but also one of those types who could manipulate the situation to get anything he wanted.

"I see you thinking, Kenni bug." Poppa swept his way across the floor to my desk. He looked down at the initial paperwork I'd started for the murder investigation.

"Since the wedding was at noon and the reception to follow, Tibbie said there wasn't any reason not to have it, and well, there's no reason for me and you to both be here." I knew there wasn't enough evidence to hold Bradley, and I didn't expect his lawyer to offer anything but to get him out of here, which meant literally he'd go free as soon as the lawyer walked through the door.

My eyes slid across the room to the door as though his release was playing out.

There'd not be any sort of initial autopsy from Max Bogus unless he worked through the night, and even at that I wouldn't get a fax until morning.

"You gonna behave if the sheriff leaves?" Betty pulled up her reader glasses and looked overtop them.

"If this isn't a joke, then I have no other option, do I?" Bradley's response made Betty's nose curl as though she'd smelled a polecat.

"Kenni, you go on. I'll be just fine." She nodded. "But next week the Women's Club has a meeting during the afternoon, and I'd like to take off for that."

"Of course you can. You don't have to work tonight to take off. You know that." I flipped the case's envelope up and put it on Scott's desk. "Besides, Scott should be back with some evidence bags, and he can stay."

"We'll see," she said and went back to eating.

I walked over to her, leaned down, and whispered into her ear so Bradley didn't hear. After all, I didn't want him to think I was really a good guy in this particular instance.

"See if Bradley wants something to eat, and get Bartleby to fix him up something." Even though Bradley was a suspect and at this time my only suspect, he was still human and needed to be treated as such.

"What was that?" Bradley asked when I grabbed my belongings and started to the door. "Did you whisper for her to come clean about this prank when you walk out?" He had a big smile on his face, looking back and forth between me and Betty.

I let go of a long sigh before I walked out into the dreary, dusky night, thinking to myself that this was going to be one long case to solve.

CHAPTER SIX

"Hello," I called into Tibbie's house when I walked in the front door.

The chatter I'd first heard when I walked in had stopped. I took a couple of steps into the entry and looked into the room on the right.

On euchre nights Tibbie turned the sitting room into the eating room. And I'd never seen this entire group of women stop eating and talking before, even when I'd previously walked into a room.

I was met with an eerie silence. Other than while drinking a good glass of sweet iced tea, I'd never seen half of these women's lips stop flapping.

Ever.

"I guess that's one way to make an entrance." Mama's dissatisfied sigh dripped out of her mouth as she set down the plate of goodies she'd brought for the game on the table. "Honey, we didn't expect to see you here since you've insisted on being the sheriff in Cottonwood."

Mama wore the sweet smile on her face as she hurried across the room to greet me.

"I mean, I guess the killer is safe and sound at the jail." Mama curled her arm in mine, giving it a little squeeze I knew very well.

I wasn't too old for the squeeze. She'd done it all my life when she wanted me not to embarrass her.

"It's all good." I looked at her as she snapped her eyes at me. I whispered, "I guess you've not taken to the bed."

"Now." She was good at ignoring, not just today but every day, when it came to what I wanted to do. She pulled out a tube of lipstick nestled in the front pocket of her pants and slipped it into my hands like no one was looking.

Joke was on her. All eyes were still on me.

"Why don't you go freshen up and wash your hands." She patted me on the arm. "I'm sure all that police stuff you've been doing has left you famished."

"I'll get the tables all set up." Tibbie Bell finally took the initiative to come save me. "Can we talk?" she asked when she passed by.

"Sure." I put the lipstick in my pocket, since Mama's hot-pink color wasn't something I wanted on my lips just when I was going to go get a big square of Lulu's lemon bars. I didn't see them on the table in the other room, but I could smell those suckers from a mile away.

Tibbie and I left everyone to mingle around the food tables to go into the room just across the hall where she'd already set up the card tables with four chairs, a deck of cards, and a notepad and pen to keep score.

"Did you get that murderer off to jail?" Tibbie had gone from long, luscious hair down her back to a pulled-up ponytail. It swung side to side as her head bobbled and her eyes grew. "Because if you didn't, I'd love one minute alone with him."

She curled her hand into a fist, and her long nails dug into the palm of her hand, making even me cringe.

"And why is that?" I asked.

"Because he ruined my chances at being in *Barnwood Brides*." The tears resting on her eyelids must've been stinging at her nose, as it flared, and she sucked back a full-on cry.

"Oh, Tibbie. I'm so sorry." I gave her a hug.

"All those women in there had taken photos and posted it all on social media." She was talking about all the ladies gathered around the food table in the other room.

"I wouldn't worry about the magazine. We can fix this with the next big wedding you're doing, and I bet Edna would do a big spread in the *Cottonwood Chronicle.*" The idea of all the people at the wedding taking photos had really started to swirl around.

"*Cottonwood Chronicle?*" The tone in her voice didn't match my excitement. "Aren't you trying to sell Edna Easterly a little too hard? I know you want me to feel better and all, but Kenni."

"Actually you gave me a good tip for the investigation for the murder." Her face lit up a little. "If everyone was taking pictures, I can get a subpoena for the phones at the wedding."

"Please don't give me credit for that." She didn't show the same amount of joy I'd gotten from the idea. "This whole mess has already gotten all over town. And if you do that, then I'll never get another job again." She leaned a little to the right and glanced over my shoulder.

"Social media," Poppa said behind me. "Photos."

I looked back to see exactly where he was. He was standing right next to Toots Buford with his nose stuck into Viola White's tomato pie. Another treat I would have tonight.

"I sure do miss all this good food." He tapped his nose. "Nothing's wrong with my smeller."

"Social media." I turned back and smiled at Tibbie. "You're brilliant."

"I am?" She drew a hand up to her chest.

"Yes. There were so many cameras there tonight, including *Barnwood Brides,* right?" I wanted to make sure what Poppa had mentioned and what I was thinking was right.

"Yes. One really good one of the dead body underneath the tablecloth." She put her hand up to her head. "What are you going to do to help me save my business?" She put her hand on her hips, her hazel eyes bearing down on me.

"First and foremost, I need to worry about this murder and getting it solved. With that will come out how you had nothing to do with it. I'll make sure it's in my statement." I wasn't sure, but somehow I'd help her.

"The caterer too?" She was pushing it. "She's had clients drop too. Thinking it's the food that was poisoned."

"Clearly the umbrella sticking out of him was the cause of death." It didn't take an autopsy report from Max Bogus to tell me that did have something to do with the man's demise. "I guess he could've been poisoned then stabbed."

There was a real need for clarification because I didn't need Tibbie going around Cottonwood saving her business by telling people that I said it was the umbrella that stopped Gary's heart.

Tibbie had a funny look on her face before she gave a slight shrug.

"Do you know something about the murder? Did you see anything?" I asked.

She looked baffled. Unable to answer my question.

"Let's just wait for the autopsy to confirm, and then we can make a plan." I told her and as I tried to keep my personal life out of my sheriff's business, but in a small town like Cottonwood, it was hard to do.

"Fine. But I want to know the minute you hear," she demanded.

"About those umbrellas," I asked just as the ladies came into the room with their plates so we could get our card game started.

"Kenni, you never made mention about my hair." Ruby fluffed her bright-red hair with the edges of her fingers. "I got a different shade of red tucked into the roots a little."

"Nice. Is that a new technique Tina is using these days?" I asked about Tina Bowers, the owner of Tiny Tina's, the local hair salon in Cottonwood.

There was more than hair being twisted in Tiny Tina's. Gossip swirled around in there, and over half wasn't even true. I'd always thought whoever made and produced hair products put some sort of scent in the liquids that made women want to spill their guts.

Euchre night was no different. Literally I could sit here all night, play my hand, and just listen. Somewhere between all the chatter would be truth that I would use to sift through to get a lead here and there. Tonight wasn't any different. I was going to listen in for any sorts of arguments that might've taken place with Gary or even with Bradley.

"Well." Ruby's lips pursed. She'd definitely not changed her signature orange lipstick to match that hair of hers. "If you'd like to get your hair done, I've got an appointment on Monday that I'd scheduled just in case I didn't like this new look, but now that I've gotten so many compliments, I don't need it."

Her eyes drew up and around my honey-blond hair. My golden highlights weren't too golden, since I was much overdue for a color and a cut.

"Maybe." I shrugged, not committing, since I wanted to see what I could gather here before I let Tina get her hands into my hair, which she was always dying to do. "I'll let you know."

It was then I noticed Ruby shift her eyes to look at Mama, who was standing a few feet away, looking pleased. No doubt she'd put Ruby up to getting me to the salon.

"Thank you, Mama. I'm an adult now. I think I know when I need to go get my hair done. It's finding the time." I shook my head and headed over to the table where my partner was sitting.

"You have to make time for upkeep. Kenni, you aren't getting any younger. Finn is a good-looking man. He won't be on the market for long." Mama was so old-school. She wanted to have grandchildren so bad, and the first step was to make me a bride.

"That he is." There was no need to ruin anyone's night by fussing with Mama.

My relationship with my dad was so much easier. He didn't try to force me to try out for cheerleading when I was in high school or run for any silly office. He accepted me for the tomboy I truly was and had taken me to hunt with him and his friends. He even took me to his hunting club meetings and his little Saturday trips to the local diner, where he met up with these friends.

Today that was Ben's Diner located downtown. I swear Dad has name etched in one of the stools at the counter, where he spent most of his mornings these days.

I looked around and saw euchre partners Mama and Viola ready to play against Gina Kim and Katy Lee Hart. They were about to start their first hand. Mama was shuffling the cards like nobody's business like it was her business.

"Cut your luck." Mama arched a sly brow and dared poor Gina to cut the deck of cards. Gina gave a low grunt before she shook her hand to gesture "no."

With that, Mama wasted no time as she started to pass the cards out in her usual way. She rounded the table, giving each player two cards, then made another round where she distributed three cards before she flipped over the top card of the cards left in the deck, which might be the would-be trump if someone called it up.

"Hey. Sorry I'm late." Jolee Fischer, my euchre partner, had finally gotten there. "It's been a crazy day."

Jolee was dressed in a pair of overalls with a light dusting of flour down the front pocket. Her blond hair was braided on each side.

"Yeah. I missed you at the wedding." I wanted to jump in to ask her why she hadn't been there.

"I heard the big news. Sorry I missed it." Her green eyes danced with a sparkle as the freckles along the bridge of her nose grew along with the smile.

"Yes!" The bangles on Viola's wrist jingled as she cheered on Mama for taking a trick. "I got the next one!"

"Who's our opponent?" Jolee looked around at the tables and noticed the two empty chairs at our table.

"I think it's Tibbie and Myrna Savage." I nodded toward the two of them coming toward us.

"I have no idea what I'm going to do with all of those flowers. Looks like the sheriff has ruined both of our businesses." Myrna and Tibbie had to be talking about the wedding reception. "Oh, Kenni."

Myrna hadn't noticed me sitting there.

"I'm sorry, Myrna. I have to do my job." I was kinda sick and tired of everyone blaming Gary's death on me. "I'm sorry this has ruined everyone's expectation of what *Barnwood Brides Magazine* was going to do for everyone's business, but I assure you that I'll do everything I can within the arm of the law to make it right."

"I'd never hurt your feelings in the world." Myrna took the chair to my left and Tibbie took the chair to my right, opposite her partner. "I voted for you to get in office, and I'd do it again, but sometimes it's best to..."

"Best to roll the body out and let the party continue?" My brows winged up. "Let everyone walk all over any evidence that will lead to an arrest so Gary's family can have some sort of peace with his passing? No. I can't do that."

From across the room, I heard Mama clearing her throat. Her not-so-subtle way of telling me to put a lid on it.

"And I'm not here to talk about business. I'm here to have some downtime while I wait on a lawyer to show up for his client at the department." I picked up the cards Tibbie had dealt in front of me.

Something was going right for me tonight. My hand included the left and right of the suit Tibbie had flipped over, along with the ace, king, and nine.

"Pick it up," I told Tibbie as Jolee gasped across from me—her way of saying she had zero of the trump I'd called. I arranged my hand with the two trump cards, ace, and king with the nine on the far right. "I'm going alone."

"Thank you, Jesus!" Jolee hollered, throwing her cards on the table before she got up. "I'm going to get some food."

"Here you go, ladies." I laid down all four cards while they threw down any trump cards they might have, then I laid down the nine since I knew they were out of any trump cards, which meant I took all the hands played, giving me and Jolee the win.

"Maybe my night will get better after all." I had some high hopes.

As the night went on, the talk of the wedding and very little talk about the murder had died down. Poppa had ghosted off somewhere, and I'd not seen him in a while.

Within a few hours, I'd started to feel somewhat normal again. Food, chatter, and some laughs were exactly what I needed before the next forty-eight hours of my life. I knew I would be digging deep into the life of Gary Futch and images of Jasmine and Dickie Dee's wedding.

"Kenni, I'm so glad to see you here," Lulu said when we met in front of the dessert table. "I want you to take that handsome young man of yours some of my chess bars."

Finn fell head over heels in love with all things Southern when he first moved to Cottonwood. That included Lulu's chess bars.

She brought them to everything. Weddings, funerals, wakes, baby showers, farmer's market, any sort of fundraiser. It was her claim to fame in the Henny Hens circle—not a title to take too lightly.

Food, or more importantly, the unequivocal love from the community for someone's recipe, was a mark of fame around here. Several women have tried to duplicate Lulu's chess bars, and all have miserably failed. She was still the reigning queen of the dessert table.

While she was sweet, Mama was more along the lines of savory with her many in-demand casseroles. And when someone outside of the Henny Hens tried to duplicate one of their recipes, oh Lordy, Mama and them would peck them to the death.

"Don't forget to remind me to give them to you before you leave." Lulu pulled her shoulder up to her ears and winked before she rushed off to talk to a few of the other ladies.

"I'm telling you, I heard him cussing someone." I looked over to see who was talking. It was Stella from Mama's church circle. She was talking to Vita Jones and Tibbie. "I heard him saying that he'd take care of it. I was waiting to see if it was going to be one of those things you see all over social media where they get up and do one of them dances all together."

"A flash mob?" Tibbie questioned.

By this time I'd turned my body away from them and nibbled on the chess bar so I didn't appear to be eavesdropping.

When I did that, I couldn't hear the full conversation. Nonchalantly I took a few steps backwards and casually turned around right before I got into close proximity of them.

I slowly turned and reached my arm out toward the platter of pigs in a blanket.

"Don't you dare." Mama smacked my hand away.

"Where did you come from?" Over the years I'd prided myself on the ability to assess a room and everyone in it, and I had to say that Mama had been nowhere near the food table. "You're like a stealth ninja."

"That's right. I'm keeping my eye on you." Her face crinkled up. "No matter how it happened, you caught that bouquet, and in all of the weddings I've been to, there's the tried-and-true saying about whoever catches the bouquet is the next one down the aisle." Mama reached over the vegetable tray and used the tongs to pluck out a carrot. "Here."

"I've never liked carrots." I snarled at the orange stick.

"That's why you have bad eyes." Mama was now just making stuff up.

"I don't have bad eyes. Twenty-twenty," I noted with pride and decided to take my chances on another shot at grabbing one of the pigs in a blanket. "Score!" I yelled and popped it into my mouth before Mama could fight me for it. "What is wrong with you?"

"I could ask you the same thing, Kendrick Lowry." Mama's use of my full name was a sure sign she was up in arms about something.

"Are you honestly upset because I'm not married?" I put my hand on my hip and stared at her. My mouth was slightly open because I couldn't believe she'd take it to this length.

"I'm not getting any younger." She tapped the back of her fingers up underneath her chin before she ran them across her forehead where she'd taken to getting Botox, which she claimed was for migraines, but I think you had to go to a real doctor for that type of Botox.

Tiny Tina's was no doctor's office, last time I drove past the salon during my daily safety drives through Cottonwood.

"More importantly, you aren't, either." She dragged her finger to jab me in the arm. "Don't you get it? Finn is a virile young man. There are several young and available women who want to take care of a man such as Finn."

"If he wants to be taken care of"—I snorted, because I knew Finn and what he liked most was the independence our relationship afford him, where we were exclusive but not hovering over each other—"then he's with the wrong Lowry. Last I checked, you're taken."

Mama's mouth dropped, and her eyes widened. She was literally at a loss for words.

I took pleasure in this odd behavior of hers, since it was rare to stump Vivian Lowry.

Her mouth popped up, a grunting noise like she was about to say something, but it didn't come out of her before she gave up and stormed away from me. I enjoyed a couple more pigs in a blanket.

I turned my ears back to the conversation between Stella, Tibbie, and Vita. This time I was slightly closer.

"Was it the groomsman they were calling for to make the toast?" Vita asked with a hint of wonder.

"Ye-yus." Stella's Southern twang came out in agreement. "One of them. But then they started the toasts, so I took a seat. That's when I looked back and noticed he'd taken the phone call outside. It only made sense it was him. You know, the one they were looking for to make a toast."

Was she talking about Bradley? Was he on the phone? And if so, who was he telling he'd take care of it? Did he take care of the waiter?

"Forget it." I popped around and smiled, becoming a fourth in their little circle. "Did you say you saw one of the groomsmen on the phone right before the waiter was found?"

I just decided to ask Stella directly before I lost my opportunity to question any of them.

She was in midmotion with her spray cheese on top of a butter cracker. She closed her mouth and casually reached across me as if none of us noticed and put the cracker back on the silver tray with the other crackers.

"I'm not sure if I should be talking about this here." Stella brushed her hands together, and with shifty eyes, she looked at the other two.

"I would appreciate any information you have that might lead me to a suspect so the victim can have some sort of peace." My phoned chirped. I pulled it from my pocket. "Excuse me, I need to take this."

I headed toward the hall to take the phone in somewhat privacy.

"That was good timing," I heard Stella say with some relief.

Stella was a nice lady, and she never steered away from gossip, but when it came time to turn the gossip into fact, a lot of them didn't want to talk to me. Like Poppa used to tell Daddy about Mama's tales, "Boy, you've got to cut whatever Viv tells you in half. In that half is where you'll find some truth to the tale she was speaking of."

Regardless, it was seared into my head that Stella had seen something, and I would get to the bottom of it.

"Hey, Scott," I answered the phone.

"Hey, Sheriff. I found out the victim's name and some personal things on him from the caterer. I'm down at the department to fill out my report, and the suspect's lawyer is here."

"What's he saying?" I opened the door to walk out on Tibbie's front porch.

"He wants his client to be released unless we are going to charge him with something." Scott and I both knew we didn't have sufficient evidence to keep him for even a few hours. "I can stall a little bit with the proper paperwork. What do you want me to do?"

Poppa's silhouette stood next to the Wagoneer.

"We'll be there in a minute." I knew Poppa had something to say by the way he was standing.

I'd seen it a million times before. It was a little game we liked to play when I was a little girl and even up until he died.

The little game of what-if, where he would bounce off me scenarios of the crime, and I'd start giving theories by answering his questions. Most of the time it didn't solve the crime, but it did give us some great places to start.

"We?" Scott asked.

"Me." I laughed it off, knowing I wasn't doing a good job covering up the fact Poppa was a ghost and no one could see him. "For a second I was thinking Duke was with me." Good excuse, and Scott fell for it, so I let it go.

"Weee-doggy, Kenni bug." Poppa ghosted into the truck. "We've got a hot one on our hands."

The pleasure of a good case always showed on Poppa's face. He loved a good puzzle, and this was turning out to have more pieces than I liked.

I turned the engine, bringing the old Jeep to life. I pulled the old gear shift to Drive and looked back at Tibbie's house. I'd not even told anyone I was leaving.

I pushed down on the gas and gave one more glance to where Mama was standing on the porch, shaking her head. She knew all too well I was going to go to the department for a long night and even longer day tomorrow.

CHAPTER SEVEN

Tibbie's house was located off the town branch, which was just a street over from Main Street. It was probably quicker for me to walk there instead of drive to the department.

Darkness had covered the town, and the glow of the carriage lights that dotted downtown were the only lights besides the Wagoneer's headlights.

For a spring night, there was a chill that hung in the air. A light breeze fluttered through the open windows, leaving a trail of goose bumps along my arm.

The excess water from the rain that'd fallen over the hanging baskets of the carriage lights ran out of the bottom of them like a faucet, giving the spring florals a really good drink of water.

"At least the rain has stopped," I told Poppa as I turned down the alley in back of Cowboy's Catfish. "Why does it always seem to rain when someone dies?"

Poppa didn't say anything.

"Is there anything to that?" I asked him. "You're up there when you're not here, right? Next time do you mind asking the Big Guy?"

"Now, Kenni, you know I can't discuss the afterlife with you." Poppa had made some sort of rule in his ghostly form with the main man in the sky where he couldn't tell me nothing and was only here to assist me so I was to stay safe. "I guess we won't have time to come up with some quick scenarios, but if you're up for it, then I've got an idea once we get in there."

Poppa changed the subject. He had a plan. I could always count on him to have a plan.

"I'm up for anything and any ideas. As long as we can keep someone else safe, you know I'm ready." It was so nice to have him here even if it was my secret to keep. "You and I both know that when the sun comes up, that office is going to be under fire."

There was no doubt in my mind Mayor Ryland, along with Edna Easterly and any other sort of media that wanted to cover a homicide once it got out about Gary Futch, would be standing either on the sidewalk outside or dead in the middle of Cowboy's Catfish to get a chance to even shout out questions.

There was a fancy luxury car practically parked in front of the door of the department.

Since the quick drive didn't give me and Poppa too much time play our little game, I knew we would be sure to do it after everyone left for the night.

"Here we go." I shoved the gear shift to Park.

"Not before you put that on." Poppa's eyes shifted to the back seat, where my sheriff's coat with my badge pinned to the front was laid across. "Always gotta remind them who's in charge."

He was right. Always right.

It was hard being a sheriff, but a woman sheriff came with much greater challenges, and in no uncertain terms Poppa was telling me that I was going to have to play hardball. There was not an opportunity to ask him how he knew because he'd already wisped out of the truck and I assumed was inside.

I reached behind me to grab my coat and tugged it on when I got out. It didn't look all that great with the dress I was still wearing from the wedding, but now that Finn wasn't working with me, I didn't really care too much what I looked like.

"Evening." I was surprised I'd not walked into a bunch of arguing. "Looks like we are having a social supper."

Betty, Scott, Bradley, and a woman who I assumed was the lawyer all sat inside of Bradley's cell, eating a big plate of Bartleby's fried chicken breasts. Something I rarely was able to score because it was so high in demand.

"Order up!" Bartleby's voice boomed through the door before he even entered the department. "Order going back," he yelled and did a quick one-hundred-eighty turn when he saw I was now there.

"You must be Sheriff Lowry." The attorney got to her feet and waited for Scott to unlock the door and let her out.

Shortly thereafter, Scott and Betty joined us on the outside of the cell while Scott locked Bradley inside.

"You don't need to do that." The attorney wagged her finger at Scott. "Now that the sheriff is here, we can clear up this entire misunderstanding, and we will be leaving. If not, we will be filing a suit against you, you, and the sheriff that will go in conjunction with the suit already filed by Jasmine Dee's father, Evan Burch."

"You've got to be kidding me!" Poppa spat in disbelief.

"Sheriff." The lawyer's steely gaze assessed me.

"Sheriff Lowry." I walked over to her with my arm outstretched to gesture her to take a seat in front of my desk.

"Can I interest you in a piece of fried chicken?" She was one of those lawyers who so loved to play a cat-and-mouse game. I could smell them a mile away. "If not, we'd love to get Mr. Fry to get us a to-go sack, along with that plate of cornbread he hurried out of here with. It seems like everyone around here is scared of you." She leaned in a little and whispered, "I'm not. Now let my client go, or I'll for sure be filing a suit first thing in the morning."

"Tomorrow is—" I was about to say Sunday.

"I know where the judge lives." She wasn't about to be let me think she was anything less than serious on her word.

"Did she say somethin' about a lawsuit with that bride?" Poppa's lips turned in, his wide nose flared with anger. "That just burns me up," he griped.

"I want him to answer a few questions for me before you take him." No way was I going to let the two of them waltz right out of this department without a few questions. I needed answers to satisfy me.

The lawyer swiveled her head to look back at the cell, where Bradley gave her a slight nod.

"Janice Gallo." She whipped out a business card and tossed it on my desk.

"Are her kinfolk Reggie and Caroline Gallo?" Poppa got really close to Janice. "I do see a smidgen of resemblance. Ask her, Kenni bug."

"Are you related to Reggie or Caroline Gallo?" I asked and noticed a tiny gesture of softening in her eyes.

"They were my parents." She eased back into the chair. There was bit of curiosity dancing in her eyes.

"Lordy be, I go way back with her people." Poppa smacked his leg in delight. "Tell her that."

I hesitated.

"Go on, Kenni, tell her." Poppa sat his ghost tushy on the edge of my desk, between me and Janice, with his arms folded across his chest.

"My grandfather knew your people. I spent a lot of time with him. He was sheriff, and he used to talk about your parents." I was always uneasy to tell anything Poppa told me, but in this case I needed to find a common thread with her to get her to break just enough to see my side of why I was holding Bradley.

Plus the fact she mentioned a lawsuit involving Jasmine Dee was not news I wanted to hear. Surely if the facts came to light, she'd be able to talk that crazy bride down.

"That's nice, but it's not going to take away the fact you are holding my client for no reason. Now, I'm asking as nice as I can for you to let him go. Now that I've had time to sit here and think, we would like to make an appointment to come back and give a statement." She put her arms on each arm of the chair and pushed herself to stand. "Deputy, you can let him out now."

"Kenni?" Scott looked at me for the answer.

"You changed your mind in the thirty seconds?" I was curious how we'd gone from exchanging business cards to Poppa knowing her family to abruptly leaving.

"It took me that long to realize you're the granddaughter who put my parents in jail for life and put me in an orphanage."

CHAPTER EIGHT

"That went well." I tapped the steering wheel with my hand as I talked to an empty car on my way down Main Street. "You could've told me you arrested her family for illegal moonshining back in the day. It was the least you could've done!"

I screamed into the air.

"Of course," I whispered.

Ghost Poppa had gotten good at disappearing when he got into hot water—A luxury I didn't have and couldn't afford at this point.

After Janice had threatened me a second, then third time with the lawsuits, I let Betty Murphy make an appointment with Janice and Bradley for tomorrow. At least they were going to come in on a Sunday.

Scott and I had decided to just call it a night and come back an hour before Janice was bringing Bradley so we could discuss all of Gary Futch's particulars. Even try to come up with some other possible suspects by digging into his life.

It'd been a full day, and I was too tired to give the case the necessary attention it was going to need. With Janice holding a lawsuit over my head, there was no room for errors. Not that I ever did have any of those issues, but this time there couldn't even be the possibility.

I turned down Broadway Street, where I owned a little cottage on the south side of Cottonwood known as "Free Row."

Living on "Free Row" wasn't exactly everyone's cup of tea in Cottonwood. And by everyone, I mostly meant Mama. She had tried everything in the world to sell the cottage house after Poppa had willed it to me.

That's what I loved most about living on "Free Row." Him and the memories we shared there.

Yeah, there were cars in the front yard propped up on cement blocks, ripped-up couches on porches, and maybe an unruly teenager or two—who didn't think I knew they were unruly—but I gave them the stare-down if I saw them outside to put a little fear in them. No one on Free Row ever bothered me, or they knew I'd be loading more than my washer and dryer.

I pulled into the driveway and noticed I'd not left a light on for Duke. Poor guy. I hadn't even thought to ask my neighbor, Mrs. Brown. Duke loved her, and he did keep her company since she was elderly and lived alone.

Too late now.

Duke wasn't in the front window with his nose pressed against it, and the blinds were still hanging. Something was strange.

Quietly I got out and opened the back door so I could get out my twelve-gauge from underneath the bench seat. Call me paranoid. When Duke was home alone, and he wasn't waiting at the window, and the blinds were still hanging, there was something off.

Slowly I walked up the drive, staying close in the shadows outside of the moon's glow.

The loud and low hound-dog bark echoed from my backyard before I'd even gotten to the gate.

"Kenni?" A sigh of relief settled in my gut when I heard Finn call my name.

"Yeah! I'll be right there!" I called and hurried back to the truck to put the shotgun back in and grab the flower bouquet I'd been whacked on the head with.

When I made it back to the gate, Finn and Duke were patiently waiting, one with a huge smile and the other with his tongue sticking out of his mouth.

"Look at my two big boys," I joked and tossed the bouquet on the ground so I could give both of them a scratch on the head overtop the fence. That was enough for Duke. He pushed his front paws off the fence and took off into the darkness.

Finn looked at the bouquet and snickered.

"I hate to tell you, but there's some videos on the Cottonwood Community social media page where that bride is whacking you with that bouquet."

"Great," I groaned and swiped the bouquet off of the ground.

"I got you a beer." Finn opened the gate and took me into his arms. "I thought you could use it. So I used my key to let Duke out, and I fed him."

I held the bouquet up to my nose. It actually smelled pretty good.

"Thanks. You are too good to me." I gave that I'm-going-to-be-fine grin and looked up into his big brown eyes. I tapped the flowers on his chest. "Too good to me."

"I love you. I'd do anything for you." He ran a finger along my cheek.

"Where's the suit? You looked so good today." I changed the subject. All that mumbo-jumbo marriage talk from Mama made my stomach hurt.

"I couldn't wait to get that thing off." He cradled my chin with his finger and thumb before he gave me a soft kiss on the lips. "Want to talk? Or you need to hit the sack?"

"I can stay up for a little bit. This homicide is going to be a pain in my you-know-what." We walked over to my back patio, where Finn had his little cooler of beer he'd brought down from his house.

He'd bought a house on Free Row a few houses down and also inherited a cat, Cosmo, who he ended up taking in after we arrested someone for murder and the cat had no place to go.

He had a sensitive side to go with those good looks. The entire package. All six foot of him.

"You want to talk about it?" He sat down and opened the cooler. He took out two beers and used the bottle opener to pop off the lids, then handed me one.

I took it and sat down in the chair next to him, tossing the flowers on the table.

"There's a lot of things that bug me about Bradley. And I'm not sure if it's the fact he's so smug, and he thinks he's so great, that makes it seem like he'd be one to kill the waiter, or the fact I overheard him talking about the groom getting his sloppy seconds that makes me think he's a jerk." I took a swig of the beer.

"Those things don't point to him as the killer." Finn glanced over at me with duck lips.

"Right, but Gary Futch, my victim, was stabbed with one of those umbrellas, and Bradley was the only one who was seen outside without an umbrella right before Gary was murdered." I knew it didn't make a lot of sense when I said it out loud, but in my head I felt like these pieces fit together somehow.

In time, I told myself. Time was the hard part, and everyone in law enforcement knew the first forty-eight hours were the most precious in any investigation.

"Where are you going with this?" Finn asked.

"I don't know. I really want to know what he meant by sloppy seconds. I want to know what he did with the umbrella. I want to know if he had any fights with Gary. Anything that would tie him to the murder." It was so early in the investigation, I knew I wasn't going to be able to solve it while sitting here drinking a beer. "I'm just going to sit here and enjoy the silence with you and Duke."

I reached over and took Finn's hand.

"How was your night?" I asked him.

Finn had recently taken the sheriff's job in the neighboring town of Clay's Ferry. Their department was in an actual building of their own with a lot more deputies and dispatch compared to my one Scott and one Betty. Finn could go into work at nine a.m. and get home by five p.m. That's how much help he had. He even his own forensic department, where I had to use a lab on the border of Clay's Ferry and Cottonwood.

"You know. Cosmo wanted a bunch of treats." He continued to talk about his night, but it was only background noise to all the rattling going on in my head.

I had so many more questions. I didn't even know if the umbrella stuck through Gary was in fact the one Tibbie had given to Bradley.

"Kenni. Earth to Kenni." Finn's hand waved in front of my face. "I'm not sure if you heard a thing I said, but Duke has been pawing at you for attention for the last minute, and you were nowhere near recognizing it." He stood up. "Which I know this activity all too well." He leaned down and gave me a kiss on my cheek. "Good night. Try to not sit up and solve the case tonight. Get some sleep."

"I'm sorry." I reached in front of me and ran my hands down Duke's fur. "Pick me up for church?"

"We are going to church?"

"Mmhmmm. Mama will be so happy." I smirked, but truthfully I wanted to get in front of Preacher Bing and a few of the auxiliary women to pick their brain on what they'd seen.

It was getting late, and Finn was right. I needed to get in bed and start fresh in the morning.

"Let's go to bed, Duke," I hollered, since he'd decided to do another fast lap around the fenced-in yard to tide him over until the morning.

I held the back door for him, and on the run past the table, he'd jumped up and grabbed those darn flowers.

"Good boy!" Poppa called, ghosting himself from the darkness of the yard to the patio. He was laughing so hard.

"You get in here too," I told him and shut the door behind me. "That's not funny," I said and looked down at Duke standing next to the kitchen table with the bouquet in his mouth as he sat so still, looking at Poppa.

He loved Poppa as much as I did. Rightfully so. Poppa had bought Duke for me as a present. The best present ever.

"Give me that." I jerked the flowers out of Duke's mouth and headed over to the kitchen cabinet to retrieve a milk-glass flower vase that'd been there a long time, years before me, from underneath the sink.

I turned on the sink faucet and filled up the vase while I heard Poppa and Duke behind me playing.

"What if Bradley and Jasmine had dated before?" I turned the faucet off and put the vase on the sill of the window. "I heard him say 'sloppy seconds.'" I pushed the bouquet into the vase, satisfied with how it looked.

"And to take it a step further, he and the bride were caught in some sort of situation by the waiter. Bradley didn't want it to come out, so he killed him." Poppa and I started our little back-and-forth.

"What could the waiter have seen that Bradley and Jasmine didn't want to come out and was so bad to kill him for?" I wondered, to add to the theory.

"There were a lot of people there. Going back to the cameras. Did someone catch anything on film? Other than you getting pelted by those flowers." Poppa's gaze passed my shoulder to look at the vase. "That was funny."

"Not too." I gave him a flat look.

"A little." He held his fingers up about an inch apart.

I started to laugh.

"It wasn't at the time, but looking back, I can't believe she came at me like that." I smiled.

"There's my little firecracker." Poppa always knew how to turn my mood around. "Now, what do you say we get some shut-eye and start fresh in the morning. Not only are you going to be busy getting everyone's phones from them, or sweet-talking them into showing you their phones, you're gonna have one crazy bride and her father, plus Viv."

"Mama?" I asked, not following him.

"When you show up in church tomorrow, she just might have a heart attack. Especially if you take that boy." Poppa rolled his eyes.

"Now Poppa. You know I love Finn. There's going to come a time I'm going to have to tell him about you." It was getting harder and harder for me to conceal my conversations with Poppa when Finn was around.

It always seemed like Finn would walk in at the moment Poppa and I had really made some headway in cases.

"I've made the excuse more than enough that I'm talking things out loud."

"You also know that you can't have both of us." Poppa's grim reality washed sadness all over me.

CHAPTER NINE

The Cottonwood First Baptist Church, located downtown, wasn't just any church. It was more of a social few hours than anything. It's where you showed off your best clothes, and as Mama would say, your Sunday go-to-meeting clothes. It's where you fix your hair, put on makeup and jewelry. You mustn't forget the jewelry.

Again, as Mama would say, it's the spit polish to any outfit.

And it was where all the gossip for the week would start. That gossip would trickle down as Sunday dragged on and filter right on into the week. That would be what the talk of the town would be about, and then come next Sunday, they'd find something different to gossip about.

This week I was particularly interested in the gossip sure to be swirling around about the murder of Gary Futch.

Boy, I was counting on hearing what everyone had to say, since pretty much ninety percent of the Cottonwood population had been invited, gone, and taken pictures. But who took snapshots of not only my only current suspect, Bradley Ines, but also any photos of the waiter, any sort of interaction between the waiter and Bradley, or just anyone?

So when I opened my closet door, you bet I was pulling out my finest Sunday go-to-meeting clothes as well as fixing my hair up real nice-like, adding a little more color to my cheeks, and splashing on red lipstick as thick as a brick to finish off the look.

"Okay, Duke." I grabbed the light wrap I'd thrown on the chair in my room after I figured I'd need to cover my exposed shoulders from the current morning chill. I headed down the hall with Duke on my heels. "Let's go out one more time, because you can't go to church, or Mama would forget I did all of this when she noticed you."

I ran my hand down my sleeveless red dress that hit right below my knees and noticed my gams didn't look half bad, since the height of my heels pushed the muscle up a little more than my tennis shoes did.

Duke jumped and bounced over to the door. Just the mere mentioning of the word "out," and excitement spilled out of my deputy canine.

"And I'll be back to pick you up afterwards, since we've got a big interview this afternoon." Bradley and his comment about Jasmine Dee, the bride, hadn't left my mind.

Even while I tried to get a little shut-eye, images of him and the other groomsmen standing there, teasing about something having to do with his sloppy seconds, played over and over.

Duke ran to the back of the yard as fast as he could to get at the squirrel doing his balancing act along the top of the fence.

"You'll get him next time!" I hollered out to him from the screen door and couldn't stop smiling. "Maybe," I whispered and turned to the kitchen when I heard the coffeepot beep Brewed.

The slamming car door echoed from outside. I glanced up at the wall clock and knew it had to be Finn. He was always right on time and never late. Mama loved this part of Finn so much. Said he kept me in line.

I grabbed two mugs from the cabinet and watched out the kitchen window over the sink. Duke's head popped up from the grass, his ears perked up, and he looked at the gate before he bolted off in that direction.

"Good morning, buddy." Finn's voice put a smile on my face. I sure was one lucky gal when it came to him, and I knew it. "Where's your mama?" He spoke in a baby voice.

My smile grew, as did the level of the coffee in the mug I was pouring for him.

"I'm in here," I called with my mouth toward the screen door. "Do we have time for a cup of coffee?"

"I guess we do." Finn stepped inside the door, Duke nearly bowling him over to get to me for a treat. "My goodness." Finn blinked a couple of times. "You look gorgeous."

"Why, thank you, Finn Vincent." I threw a little more of my Southern accent into it. "You clean up mighty good yourself."

"What if I forgo the coffee and get a kiss or two?" He glided over, staring down at me with his big brown eyes, then kissed me.

"I should arrest you, Sheriff, for stealing a kiss and messing up my lipstick." I winked and turned back to the counter to retrieve our mugs. "Here." I pushed his mug between us when he went in for another kiss. "I can't have you messing up an investigation."

"Oh," he snickered and threw his head back. "I should've known you were doing this for the job and not me."

"Are you saying that I don't look this great all the time?" I asked.

"To me I like you best with none of this on, but sometimes it's nice to see you all. . ." He didn't seem to have the word for it as he wiggled the fingers on his left hand in front of my face. "Are you sure your mama is going to survive you coming into the Baptist church looking like this?"

"Sunday go-to-meeting clothes." I adjusted the knot in his tie.

"Your meeting clothes are some fancy duds." Duke wasn't going to stand there any longer waiting for a treat. He shoved his big head between me and Finn, hitting right at Finn's free hand. "Sorry, buddy."

Finn gave him a good scratch, opened the treat jar, and flipped Duke a treat.

"What exactly is your plan, so I know what to do?" Finn asked.

"My plan is to listen to the gossip. Then I want to figure out who took some really great photos of the reception." I took a few sips of coffee as I walked over to the screen door and locked it and then the main door.

"I'm sure there won't be any shortage of that." Finn picked up my wrap and my phone off the counter.

"Thank you." We took a couple quick sips before we headed out the front door to his Dodge Charger parked in my driveaway. The windows were rolled down, and the car was still humming where he'd not turned it off.

"Where are you two lovebirds heading out this morning?" Mrs. Brown was pretty much a shut-in and rarely went too many places. She stood at the edge of the property line, giving her azalea bushes a nice drink of water from the garden hose. Her nightcap was still pulled down over her hair, and her night cream was as thick as when she'd put it on.

"Church," I said while Finn hurried around me to open the door.

"Lookin' like that, child?" Her eyes drew up and down me.

"Mrs. Brown, I said the exact same thing." Finn wiggled his eyes. He shut my door and ran around the car to get in on the driver's side.

"I sure hope Preacher Bing doesn't catch you giving her the eyes." Her brows wiggled up and down. "Or anyone else, for that matter." She stuck the end of the hose deep in the bushes with one hand and waved us off in the other.

Finn and I waved bye to her. I would've asked her to join us, but it would take an hour for her to get ready, so I made a mental note to ask her on Saturday nights if she wanted to go.

The Cottonwood First Baptist Church was on the south end of town, and we took our time driving through town, going in and out of streets to get there. There was no way I wanted to get there before Polly.

The church stood off the road with about an acre between Main Street and the building itself. There was a large staircase that led up to a huge concrete-covered porch with five large pillars holding it up. Four large doors were evenly spaced along the porch that opened up into the vestibule of the church.

"Don't forget. Prayer circle is tomorrow night in the undercroft." Viola White flailed her arms, looking like a bird about to take flight right there in the vestibule with her feather boa wrapped around her neck, feathers flying everywhere.

Viola was standing in the middle of most of the auxiliary women and a few who I recognized as being in the bell choir.

"My goodness, Kenni Lowry." She rushed over. "Are you trying to show me up? Or is there some news?" Her eyes moved past my face and straight to my hand, where she was searching for a ring.

An engagement ring.

"I woke up this morning and thought I would show you up." I winked and gave her a quick hug. "I just heard you're gearing up for this week's prayer meeting."

"That's right. There's a lot to be praying for around here." She pulled me closer, but she faced the doors and gave a little smile and wave when she recognized someone. "Did you hear about Darby Gray?"

"No. What happened?" I loved going to see Darby, the owner of the inn. It was one of few places to stay when folks came to visit Cottonwood. It was located in the country, and it had a large wraparound porch that was good for sittin' and sippin' sweet tea.

"I heard at the wedding she'd fallen and broken her leg. We've got to get her to the top of the prayer list." Viola nodded a few times with her eyes all bugged open. She patted my hand. "Don't you worry. I've got you second."

"Me?" I asked. By this time, Finn had gone over to talk to some of the other members of the congregation.

The organ music filtered out of the nave, letting everyone know service was about to start.

"With all this murdering and stuff happening underneath your nose yesterday, the talk around town is maybe there needs to be some fresh blood in the sheriff's department."

"Fresh blood?" This was not the gossip I wanted to hear, and I certainly didn't want to be the talk of the town when I needed it to be about the murder.

Not me.

"Ahem." Preacher Bing cleared his throat from the doors to enter the nave. He pinched a closed-mouth grin and gave a nod through the doors.

"We will talk later. You go first so I can make my grand entrance." She gestured me ahead of her with her finger.

Now I was mad. I couldn't believe how this had gotten turned around on me.

"Uh-oh, what's wrong?" Finn was waiting inside the doors to walk down the aisle so we could take a seat in the front pew, where Mama was so proudly leaning past the side of the pew with a huge grin on her face.

"I'll tell you later," I muttered as my eyes narrowed, taking in all the whispers filtering behind me and Finn as we walked down the aisle.

"Scoot down, Ruby," Mama whispered, knocking her hips for Ruby to scoot over to make room for us. "Look at you." Mama's chin jutted forward to look at the altar with pride written all over her face. "Cottonwood got a glimpse just now. You two are going to make me real proud when you walk down the aisle in my wedding dress."

"Your dress?" I laughed.

"I've been saving it for you." She gave a long, satisfied sigh that matched the hum of the organ.

CHAPTER TEN

"You two made a very grand entrance." Preacher Bing stood in the undercroft next to the punch bowl. "I couldn't hardly keep everyone's attention for the sermon, for all the people staring at you two."

"Goodness, if something was to happen, Preacher, you'd be the first one to know, since you make everyone take premarital classes." I sipped on the delicious ice cream punch. I picked up the ladle and put it into the glass bowl, making sure I got a little bit of the ice cream.

It was a Southern staple to serve a big glass bowl of ice cream punch, even though the Presbyterians called it Presbyterian punch. I wasn't sure who came up with the combination of using 7UP, pineapple juice, frozen limeade, frozen orange juice, and a full gallon of rainbow sherbet to make up the delicious drink, but I was mighty happy to see it here today.

"Speaking of premarital classes and weddings." I looked at the preacher.

He'd been the preacher since I was a little girl. He was as scary back then as he was now. He stood well over six feet tall. His hair was plastered to his head, and his bangs hung down on his forehead. He was a lanky man who reminded me of Lurch from the Addams Family. See how I meant he was scary?

Plus he had a direct line to God, and right now I needed that since I'd yet to see Poppa anywhere around.

"When you counseled Jasmine and Dickie Dee, did you see anything unusual about the two?" I asked.

"What do you mean by unusual? Every couple is different." He stared down at me with his dark eyes, circles underneath to match.

"Any sort of arguments? Disagreements?" I asked.

"Do you think they had something to do with the waiter's death?" Preacher Bing asked.

"I'm not sure."

"Or are you upset and trying to find something to blame for the possible lawsuit they want to file against you." He shot me a glance before he lifted the glass to take another sip of the punch. His eyes glazed over the brim.

My brows knotted, and my jaw dropped.

"No. They have no grounds to sue me. She's the one who assaulted me." My nostrils flared. I downed the little punch left in my paper cup before I squeezed it tight in my hands and tossed it into the trash can.

"Oh, I saw the entire fight on social media." He smiled. "I wish people didn't put everything on there. It can be entertaining, though."

"Whose social media did you see?" If someone filmed me, it was a good possibility they got more than one fight. The waiter and his killer, for one.

"If you use hashtag-the-couple's-name, you'll find all sorts of things." Why on earth had I not thought about that? "Other than that, I'm not really allowed to tell you about the sessions I had with the young couple."

"Not without a warrant," I warned and made darn sure to remember to make good on the threat I'd just given him.

"We can't be having that." Preacher Bing knew I'd make good on my promise to get a warrant now, since I'd done it before.

"There was an issue." He paused as if he were trying to choose his words.

"Issue? Like argument? Disagreement?" I helped him along.

"Umm"—his head bobbled—"argument. Definitely an argument."

"Do you know what the argument was about?" I asked.

"Something about the bachelor party, and I didn't get into specifics. I only dealt with how they were going to handle it as a couple and if it did arise after they were married." Preacher Bing blushed.

"Are you saying he might've gone to, like, a strip club or something to that effect?" I asked, wondering if that's what Bradley had been talking about when he was in custody—calling the entire time in jail a prank and asking if they were getting back at him for what had happened.

The question lingered before I pushed it aside to make sure I used the time I did have with Preacher Bing.

"During these premarital sessions," I started to say, before I noticed the wandering eye of Mama upon me. She jerked around to talk to Ruby as if she didn't see me. "What types of things do you cover in them?"

"Are you asking for the investigation or for personal reasons?" His right brow shot up.

"You never know." I shrugged. "For now, it's for the purpose of knowing what was covered."

"First and foremost, we talk about where each of them stand in accordance with religious beliefs. We also cover things like finances. . ." His voice trailed off, the wrinkles on his forehead deepening as though he'd realized something.

"Something with finances?" I asked.

"Finances create a big stir in marriages. When we covered that part of the class, Dickie had very different ideas of how he would run the family company," Preacher Bing recalled.

"Family company?" It was the first time I'd heard anything about a family company, which would explain the huge wedding and inviting all the government officials if they were going to do something very local.

It was a whole mindset around Cottonwood business owners—you scratch my back, I scratch your back. It was the oldest trick in the book to have me over for supper or even a wedding, only to call in the time they'd invited me when they needed me to look the other way or turn the other cheek.

"Jasmine's family business, where her father has been grooming Dickie for a few years." Preacher Bing shrugged like it was no big deal. "Dickie has an idea for the company where Jasmine said it was, and I quote, stupid. That's when they got into an argument about her calling him names."

"There was already trouble in paradise." I couldn't help but think this would create some motives to not get married, but to kill a waiter to stop the wedding was a little too far-fetched for me.

"That and little white lies. Children." He said "children" in a deeper voice when he went back to rattling off what issues come up in the premarital classes. "I think the issues surrounding children take up a lot of time. And how people try to bring in how they were raised to combine with how their partner was parented. It's a tricky subject."

"Other than the bachelor party incident and the family business, you felt pretty confident they were meant to get married?" I asked, making sure there were no other reasons that might spark either to hurt the waiter. "Nothing like wedding disagreements? Or any sort of family coming together? Friends?"

"You know a bride." He pulled his lips tight. "Actually, you don't." He caught himself. "I've been around a lot of them. They never like any of the groomsmen or things they do. She did want to know the best man's speech before he was to give it, but as you noticed, he didn't even show up for the toast, and they didn't even get to finish them before—" Preacher Bing made the motion of a stab to his stomach.

"Back up." Poppa decided to join us. "Did he say she wanted to know the speech?"

"Jasmine wanted to know the speech of the best man or everyone?" I asked.

"Just the best man." Preacher Bing scratched his temple. "His name escapes me."

"Bradley Ines."

"Yes. Bradley. That's right." He nodded.

"Other than the premarital counseling, did you see anything out of the ordinary at the reception? I know you've been to so many." I reiterated how he'd mentioned he knew a lot of brides.

"I can't say there was. The music was fun. The food was delightful, and Tibbie did a fantastic job coordinating everyone, down to the little umbrellas. Nice touch." He snorted. "Always the little party planner in Sunday school when she was little. Remember that?"

My brows knotted.

"That's right. You were always down at the drugstore, trying to get a cherry soda-fountain drink. You were never on time." There was a hint of scolding in his voice. "I've got to mingle. The duty calls."

"If I have any more questions, I'll stop by." I didn't see a reason to get his statement on file, since he really didn't seem to tell me anything of great importance. The only thing I wanted to check out was the bachelor party and if anything happened there.

That was mainly for my curiosity, since the waiter was dead and not the bride or Bradley.

I walked toward Tibbie and Jolee. Both of them were in the soup-beans-and-cornbread line.

"Are you eating?" Jolee asked.

"No. My stomach is in knots. This murder has got me upside down, and knowing that I'm going to be the talk of the town this week isn't setting well."

"Good." Jolee shoved a Styrofoam bowl into my hands. "Can you get a bowl of beans for Mrs. Brown? She called me this morning and told me she didn't want to eat what Meals On Wheels had for tonight and if I'd get her some beans. You know how all these Henny Hens talk if you get seconds."

I listened to her go on.

"'If Jolee keeps eating like that, Ben will never come back to her. She'll be as big as a house. She should wait to eat like that until after she gets her a man,'" Jolee mocked.

"Speaking of Ben." It was a sore subject. Jolee and Ben Harrison had been enemies to lovers in a sense, then gone back to enemies recently. Only because Ben had broken up with her and we'd yet to know why. "Any news on that front?"

This was when I needed to flip the switch from the job to the friend. I'd steered clear of asking her last night at the euchre game because there were just too many ears around.

"I heard he's just as miserable as you." Tibbie put her two cents in. "Maybe you should talk to him."

"There's no more talking." Jolee grabbed two pieces of cornbread and headed off to get us a table.

"She didn't say anything about cornbread for Mrs. Brown." I held up two fingers for the volunteer to give me two pieces.

"Who wants to eat soup beans without cornbread?" Tibbie was right. We loved to crumble up the cornbread and mix it into the soup beans along with some cut-up onion.

Mouthwatering.

"Say, Tibbie, I was wondering about those umbrellas you had gotten for the wedding." I followed her and Jolee to an empty table next to the exit.

It was a perfect spot for me to slip away without being noticed.

"Wedding party," she stated with a mouthful of beans. "Only for the wedding party. I got them last minute down at Lulu's Boutique. After I saw what the weather was going to do, I wanted to make sure we had some on hand for when they walked out of the church."

"That was smart thinking." Jolee nodded and glanced over at the person sitting next to us. "I didn't get any punch." She pulled her shoulders back and looked up over the heads of all the people sitting at the table toward the back of the undercroft where the punch bowl was. "I'm going to get me some punch. Y'all want any?"

Tibbie and I both said we'd take a cup before Jolee scurried off.

"Lulu is pretty amazing. She came up with the wedding monogram because she's got one of those Cricket machines in her shop in the back craft area." Craft night at Lulu's Boutique was fun. She did have everything you needed to craft whatever your little heart desired.

My heart didn't desire crafts at all. I went along just to hang out with my friends. But a lot of the time I went there when Jolee's On The Run food truck was parked there. Lulu and Jolee had an agreement. While the food truck was serving food, the customers could go into the craft area in Lulu's Boutique to sit and eat.

It was a deal Jolee had worked out with a few of the area businesses after she'd gotten the town council to approve the necessary permits to operate a food truck in Cottonwood. That was one of the sore subjects between her and Ben.

"You only got twelve umbrellas, and one went right through the chest of the waiter." I sighed. "What can you tell me about Bradley and the bride?"

"Nothing but they dated back in college. That's how she met Dickie. Bradley and Dickie were best friends."

"Sloppy seconds," I whispered.

"Kenni!" Tibbie jerked up and covered her mouth. "That's terrible to say."

"I didn't say it. Bradley Ines said it."

Did Bradley Ines really believe Dickie had gotten his sloppy seconds, or did he kill the waiter to sabotage the wedding? The wedding he thought he would have with Jasmine.

It was a far-fetched theory, but at least it was a theory I could chew into when Bradley came to the department this afternoon.

About that time, Edna Easterly walked by.

"Ouch, Kenni." She groaned and jerked from my grip on her fishing jacket. "You're rude."

"I wanted to tell you how nice you looked at the wedding yesterday." I offered her Jolee's seat since Jolee had been stopped by another group of women, who didn't seem to care Jolee had her hands full with three punch cups.

"I already know what you want. Scott Lee told me at the reception yesterday you wanted all the photos off my camera." She lifted one of the many pockets on her jacket and pulled out a thumb drive. She wagged it with each word. "The only reason I'm doing this is because you've ruined everyone else's career with that little stunt of shutting down the wedding, and I'm not going down with your ship."

She smacked the thumb drive that I assumed contained all the wedding photos down on the table before she headed off in another direction.

"Why is it that everyone is mad at me for ruining the reception, when they should be mad at the waiter for getting killed or the killer for killing the waiter at the reception?" I looked across the table at Tibbie, who probably wasn't the best one to discuss this with since she was the first one who said I ruined her event-planning business. "Do you happen to have copies of the speeches from the toast?"

"I'm going to get some banana pudding." Tibbie planted her hands on top of the table and pushed herself up. "I'll see you later."

"Let's get out of here." Poppa saved me from beating myself up. "We've got wedding photos to look at."

I put my hand up on the table and got the thumb drive off before I started my search for Finn. When I glanced around the undercroft and didn't see him, I headed outside to where he was standing with most of the men discussing their favorite Kentucky Derby contender, maybe thinking about placing a wager or two.

It was spring in Kentucky, and that meant one thing. Horse racing. Soon the gossip for the women would turn to what hat they'd be wearing to the Derby while the men would discuss betting odds.

I had to strike the auxiliary women while they were hot, or I would lose my window of opportunity.

"Daddy, when is Mama's next auxiliary meeting?" I pulled Daddy aside from the men for a few minutes.

"Tomorrow night over at Vita and Luke Jones's before the town council meeting."

"Good. Two birds with one stone, Kenni bug." Poppa rubbed his hands together. "Do you think you could go back in there and get a banana puddin' to go?" Poppa watched Vernon Bishop, the president of the Cottonwood First National Bank, walk past with a big bowl of the delicious sweet.

"Kenni!" Tibbie called out to me when Finn and I were walking to his Charger. "Here."

She handed me a white binder with a slip of paper in the clear pocket on the front with "Jasmine and Dickie's Wedding" scrolled in fancy writing.

"That's their entire wedding planner. Speeches and all." Her lips drew into a thin, bird-like smile. "I'm sorry. You didn't ruin my career, but I want you to catch the SOB who did."

"Thank you." I hugged her tight.

CHAPTER ELEVEN

"What did you mean when you said sloppy seconds?" I asked Bradley once he got settled into the one of the chairs in front of my desk.

Bradley shifted. His lawyer next to him gave him the nod to answer the question. Bradley turned his chin over his right shoulder to look at Finn. Finn was sitting at Betty's desk, eating the bowl of the banana pudding I'd gotten, and Poppa was hovering over him, licking his chops.

Finn looked up and noticed us all staring at him.

"I'll be over at Cowboy's Catfish if you need me." Finn got up and took the bowl of pudding with him.

"Back to the question." I shifted my eyes from Finn to Scott and back to Bradley. "Did you date Jasmine back in college?"

"I did," he confirmed.

"What does this have to do with the murder of the waiter?" Janice Gallo asked.

Her black hair parted down the middle and was cut to her shoulders, with both sides neatly tucked behind her ears. It lay slick against her head with not one flyaway or stray. She had thick black brows and big round black eyes that didn't miss a beat.

When she talked, I tried not to stare at the small mole just above her upper lip on the right side. Mama would call that a beauty mark. Janice probably woke up like this.

I ran my hand down my hair, feeling a bit self-conscious since I'd gotten to the office right before they'd gotten there and grabbed one of the extra sheriff uniforms from the supply closet so I could change out of my Sunday go-to-meeting clothes.

"I'm just gathering facts." I gave her a flat look.

"Fine. You can answer." She jerked her chin toward him.

"Yeah. We dated, and that's how she met Dickie. It wasn't like we dated a while. Really it was like two dates, and that was it. Nothing else. She was decent enough to tell me she was going out with Dickie. I moved on to the next girl." He snickered.

I wanted to smack the grin off of his face, but then I'd not be able to slap the cuffs around his wrists when it came time.

"Did you plan the bachelor party?" I asked.

He shifted uncomfortably in the wooden chair. The chair groaned from the movement of his weight he put on the arm as his elbow leaned heavily on it.

"Sure. I was the best man." His bottom teeth raked his top lip a couple of times before he sucked in a big inhale. "That's the duty. Send the groom out of his single life with a bang."

"What did you do to send him off with a bang?" I used his own words against him.

"Again, what does this have to do with a murder investigation?" Janice asked.

Scott motioned behind their backs that he had seen something in the photos from Edna. He'd downloaded them to his computer after I got back to the office.

"I am trying to establish the frame of mind of all the people in the wedding. From what I could see even before Mr. Futch's death, there was some tension between the bride and Mr. Ines here." I sighed and flipped a page in the file. There was nothing there, but they didn't see that.

"According to the photos on this device." I picked up the thumb drive Edna had given me and showed it to them. I'd yet to have time to look through them, so I was going out on a big limb.

However, Scott had gone through a few of them and was currently printing some off.

"There were a few moments when the bride and Mr. Ines were in a heated discussion. I am wondering if it had anything to do with the night of the bachelor party or the fact that your client is still holding a flame for the one who got away and would do anything to ruin her wedding." I jerked my head to face Bradley straight on. Scott walked over and handed me the two photos. "Where Mr. Bradley"—I took the photos and just on a hope and a prayer laid them out in front of Janice and Bradley—"and the bride are in what looks like a heated discussion. Here you can clearly see the waiter standing next to them. So either your client knows Mr. Futch, or Mr. Futch heard something he didn't need to hear, and your client killed him."

I smacked the top of my desk with a flat palm.

"Which is it, Mr. Ines?" I stood up over my desk and poked my finger down on the photos. "What is going on in these photos? It sure doesn't look like the toast you was supposed to give to a happy couple."

I reached down by my feet where I'd put my purse and the wedding binder Tibbie had given me. I opened up the binder and flipped to the tab labeled Speeches. Thank God Tibbie was really good at organizing.

"Here's your speech to the happy couple. It says. . ." I picked up the paper and read straight from it, not leaving a single word out. "Ladies and gentlemen, thank you all for coming out tonight to celebrate the wedding of two people we all love, Jasmine & Dickie!

"When I first met Jasmine, I knew that she was the woman Dickie would end up marrying. Even if it hadn't dawned on him quite yet, it was obvious to everyone around just how smitten he was with her. They talk about a bride's glow, but this man was shining since the moment he met her. He changed for the better without realizing it. And we all could see it."

The more I read the speech, the more shifting he did in the chair. I didn't look at him. I just kept reading with Poppa cheering me on in the background.

"You've got him now, girl! Keep going!" Poppa was doing some uppercuts and jabs like he was training for a ghost boxing league.

"Dickie couldn't stop talking about her. We'd go out with the boys, and Jasmine's name would be brought up every two minutes. So when he came to me to tell me that he would be proposing, my only response was, 'Well, it's about time!'"

I used my best theatrical voice to play up how I thought the speech would sound if it really were heartfelt.

"Look at that smug face. Knock him in that pretty jaw, Kenni bug." Poppa had moved next to Bradley. He bent down close to Bradley so he could blow a steady stream of air toward Bradley's nose.

Bradley reached up and grabbed around it, like there was a hair hanging or something tickling it, before he rubbed it a few times.

I went on reading aloud. "There's something special about these two. They go together without forcing it. They love each other without fighting it. And they care about each other without thinking about it. She was the one from the very beginning, Dickie, and we're all so happy to be able to take part in your big day. Cheers!"

I smacked the piece of paper down in front of Janice. Scott took the papers shuffling off the fax machine. There was really only one person who ever faxed the department on a late Sunday afternoon. Max Bogus.

Poppa had ghosted behind Scott. Now both of them were reading the report.

Poppa slid his eyes across the room. There was something in them. Something telling. Something he'd seen in the report.

"Does this sound like a speech you'd give someone who was taking your sloppy seconds?" I emphasized. "This is an entire speech of lies. You know it. The groom knows it. And the bride knows it. What else could you be lying about, Mr. Ines? Did you or did you not kill Mr. Futch to ruin Jasmine and Dickie Dee's wedding because they made you look like a fool years ago, bruising that big ego of yours in front of all of those men in the wedding party? Who, by the way, have known you as long as you've known Dickie."

"This is ridiculous. There's not one single piece of evidence that my client laid a hand on Mr. Futch."

"Maybe not a hand, but the force of stabbing someone with an umbrella. Because last we checked, everyone in the wedding party had their umbrella except your client, and he was drenched along with Mr. Futch." I leaned back in my chair and folded my arms.

Bradley went to open his mouth.

"I'm sorry. I forgot you were outside vaping in the pouring rain." I reached over and picked up the cigarette I'd gotten him last night. It'd rolled over to the side of the phone. "I thought you said you didn't smoke cigarettes." I snapped a finger toward Scott. "Deputy Lee and I picked up all the cigarette butts on the venue's entire property. They are all in that bag."

Scott scrambled to go through the evidence we'd collected to be tested, and when he got to the bag, he held it up.

"Am I going to need you to give us a DNA sample?" He scoffed at my words. "If you did nothing wrong, then I don't see why you'd have a problem." I looked between him and Janice.

Playing bad cop was exhausting.

"You need to go see Max," Poppa whispered.

"As a matter of fact, Deputy Lee will follow along behind y'all while you head on down to the health department just a couple blocks over to submit." I smiled and cocked my head toward Scott. "Deputy?"

"Fine. I'm fully believing in my client, and I'm going to clear his name." Janice stood up and Bradley followed. "That's why I took this job. I'm tired of the Lowrys putting my people in jail."

"'Scuse me." Mama pushed past Janice on her way into the department. "Hello there. I am so glad I ran into you. Thank you so much for letting me borrow your umbrella at the wedding reception. I hate to say it, but I think I lost it. I put it on the table when I came in, and someone must've picked it up."

The air left my lungs.

"Looks like you have a new suspect, Sheriff." The look on Janice's face said a million words.

CHAPTER TWELVE

"That's ridiculous." Mama scoffed on our way out the door as I walked her to her car. "The only thing I said to the waiter that might be off-color was about how he was slow, and when the sheriff gets married, we will make sure that caterer won't hire him."

"You didn't." My shoulders slumped.

"You've got all the tongues wagging about a big wedding announcement," Mama cackled, her hand dug down into her pocketbook where she searched around. "Where are those keys?"

"I'm not talking about me and Finn. I'm talking about the waiter. You didn't have an argument with him, right?" I questioned her.

"I most certainly wouldn't call it an argument, Kenni." She played it off. "Ask Viola and Ruby—they were right there. And maybe Tibbie. Or that caterer. She's the one who told him the customer is always right."

"I just overheard the fancy lawyer saying she was coming to the town council meeting tomorrow night." Poppa shifted to Mama's car. A worried look settled on his face, and I knew this wasn't going to turn out good.

"What would you call it, Mama?" I asked and bent down to get her to look at me.

"I know I threw those keys in here." She lifted the purse up to her eyes, tilting it one way and then the other to get a good look inside.

"They are on the car." Poppa pointed. "And the car is locked."

"How on earth did you do that?" I shook my head and covered my eyes, resting the sides of my hands on the driver's side window to look in.

"Do what?" Mama continued to rummage through her purse.

"Lock the keys inside." I tapped the window.

"You've got to be kidding me." She gasped and shook her head. "I have a terrible habit of hitting the lock when I get out when I come to see you. Especially when I come to the house on Free Row. I know you love that house and Finn loves living a few doors down from you, but Kenni, Poppa would want the best for you. I know." She placed her silky hand on her chest. "He was my daddy."

"Viv, there's nothing wrong with my house." Poppa's nose flared.

"If that was the case, he wouldn't've left it for me." I walked around the car and lifted up the handles to see if just one would open.

No chance.

"He left it for you to sell and have money." Her assessing eyes looked me up and down.

"Listen, you better go inside and give me a statement about the interaction between you and Gary Futch, because I have reason to believe you've now become a suspect. If not on my list, then Janice's list." I gestured to the passing car with Janice and Bradley inside.

Janice had a look of satisfaction on her face. She had something up her sleeve.

"Don't you worry yourself about that." Mama giggled. "It looks like he had more than one argument by the way it ended up."

"Mama, you're the only one who had a public disagreement with him."

"I wouldn't call it that, honey." Her brows knitted. "I guess we better call your father. He's going to have to bring me the spare key. He's not going to be happy. He wanted to go to the afternoon races. I told him that you're not supposed to gamble on the sabbath, and I swear

Preacher Bing overheard him and all those men in the parking lot planning their little rendezvous."

"Mama. Stop!" I yelled to get her attention.

"Kenni. You're screaming like a child. What is wrong with you?" She looked around as if there was someone who could have heard us.

No one was in the alley, unless you counted the mice scurrying around in the dumpster, feasting on the Cowboy Catfish's garbage.

"Do you understand no one on record had an argument with the waiter who is now dead? Stabbed with what appears to be Bradley's umbrella? No one but you." I gave her a hard look.

"But it was his umbrella. . ." Her voice fell away. She put her hand to her mouth. "Oh dear." She looked at me with the worry on her face that matched my insides. "Oh." She hooted a few times. "This doesn't look good, does it?"

"No, Mama." I took her by the elbow. "I'm going to have you go inside and give a statement to Deputy Lee because I can't take my own mama's statement." She shuffled along beside me, probably not hearing what I was saying because the worry had settled on her brows and she was looking down, gnawing on her lip. "While he is doing that, I'm going to go to the funeral home and see Max. I'll call Daddy from my car on the way over there."

I opened the door.

Scott was thumbing through all the paperwork and appeared to be getting the file for the case in order.

He watched silently while I sat Mama in the chair next to his desk. She put her little pocketbook in her lap. She sat still, looking forward but with no real focus.

I gave my head a quick tilt, gesturing for Scott to follow me.

"What are we going to do about the umbrella now?" he asked as I turned my body away from Mama so she'd not hear me, even though the department was so small it made it hard not to.

"Mama and Gary had a disagreement of sorts." I looked at Scott. The worry on his face said it all. "Right. I want Mama to give you a statement of everything. From brushing her teeth in the morning to her daily constitution."

Scott's face softened, letting me know he wasn't going to ask Mama when the last time was she went to the bathroom.

"You know what I mean. I need to know exactly when and how she got the umbrella from Bradley and hopefully get some clear answers on just how hard someone stabbed Gary with that umbrella, because Mama isn't that strong. That's the only thing we have to hang our hat on." I looked around Scott and peered at Mama. "I need to go see Viola White, Ruby Smith, and Tibbie Bell. Mama said they all heard it."

Now I knew why they were all acting so suspicious when I asked them if they'd seen anything. They had, and they didn't want to rat out Mama.

This was the longest I'd ever seen her go without talking.

"You think you can do this?" I asked.

"Yeah." He sighed.

My mind fluttered back to the church, when Viola had asked me if I had a minute right before Preacher Bing had interrupted us, and right after she'd told me there were rumors of needing fresh blood in the sheriff's department.

I couldn't help but wonder if she was going to tell me about the disagreement Mama and Gary had. I'd sure find out tomorrow when I stopped by the jewelry store to pay her a little visit. Then I wondered what time Ruby Smith's appointment was at Tiny Tina's tomorrow. Maybe I did need a little trim on the edges of my hair.

I lifted my hands up to feel the edges.

"What are you thinking?" Scott asked.

"Not sure just yet, but once you get Mama's statement, you can let her go. I'll call my dad to bring her extra car key to her." I sighed. "You and I will do a workup on the whiteboard when I get back."

I gave Mama a kiss on the forehead before I headed into Cowboy's Catfish to tell Finn my plans.

"I'll walk home." He was sitting at the bar, shooting the breeze with Bartleby. "It's a nice afternoon."

"Are you sure?" I asked.

"Don't let him fool you." Bartleby's smile held a secret.

"What?" I looked between the two men.

"I've got an apple pie coming out of the oven in a few." Bartleby told on Finn.

"Finn Vincent," I gasped. "You just ate a big bunch of banana pudding."

"I've got that sweet tooth today." He pouted in a very cute and charming way.

"Fine. I'll see you later this afternoon." I kissed him goodbye. "Send Finn home with an extra slice for me." I winked at Bartleby on my way out the front door of the diner.

I didn't want to go back through the department because Mama was in there and I didn't want to disturb her or even hear what she was telling Scott during her statement. If there was any way Janice could turn Mama's recollection of her tiff with Gary—and I was calling it a tiff—it would be how I had somehow manipulated Mama's words.

I wasn't going to let that happen, but I sure was going to go to the town council meeting and make sure I put in my two cents.

Unlike Mama, I did keep my keys in my old Wagoneer. Cottonwood residents were still able to keep their doors unlocked and keys in their cars. It wasn't like we had a high crime rate when it came to things like break-ins, and I hoped they'd felt safe enough to keep to the simple ways of life. Those were the things they needed to remember when it came to election time, not things like Gary's murder that were out of my control

When I got into the Jeep, I tuned into WCKK, the local radio station, so I could get some music in my head and Mama out of it. I needed to be as impartial as I could be, and when Max Bogus gave me details on Gary's autopsy, I needed Mama out of my head. Music did that for me.

Before I knew it, I'd pulled right on up in front of the Cottonwood Funeral Home, where the morgue was located. It was the only funeral home in Cottonwood, and since they already did have the facility in the basement to fix everyone up for their eternal slumber, it only made sense for the town to also rent the space and equipment for times such as this.

Plus there was no one better than Max Bogus to be elected as the county coroner. He had the experience as the funeral home director. Though you didn't need a medical degree to be the coroner, Max had one, so it all just came together.

It never got any easier, standing in the door of the cold, institutional-looking room, staring at the dead body lying on the stainless-steel table. My eyes took in the scene before I put on the blue gown and gloves Max had left for me at the door.

"Good afternoon." Max's voice echoed off the cold walls when I walked in. The first smell of death really did knock me for a loop as soon as I walked in. "Hairnet on the counter."

"I'm curious as to what you found out." I pulled the net over my hair, giving the top of my head a few scratches from the itchy fabric. I also plucked a paper mask from the box and kept my hand up to my nose to hold it in place to ward off the stench.

"You okay?" he asked, glancing up.

"Yeah. Fine," I said and looked around to see where Gary was. "Where's the body?"

I was expecting to see Gary lying on the surgical table with the Y cut, but the stainless table was empty and shiny.

"That's why I wanted you to come down here. I didn't want to proceed with opening him until you got a look at the X-rays you told me to make sure I took, and I'm glad I did." He waved me over to the window into the X-ray room.

When I looked in, there was Gary with the machine overtop of his lifeless body.

"It appears there was a blow to the side of his head that killed him. Pretty hard too. He was hit so hard it blew out his right pupil." He'd pulled up the X-ray to show me Gary's skull and facial features. "That wasn't the only hit. He also sustained a blow to the back of the body, which I believe caused him to go down. As for the umbrella, I think that it was outside and the killer used it on him after he was dead." He held up a finger when I opened my mouth to ask a question. "Stick with me."

If that was the case, maybe Mama had left the umbrella outside and not taken it in. Which was plausible because Mama never took an umbrella inside in fear it caused bad luck, especially not a wet one in fear it'd make a mess. Mama's house was always visitor ready from the tidiness and the coffee cake in the freezer that could never be touched because it was only there to be enjoyed by drop-in guests.

"I found some residue from the pavement on the party patio." He scanned down images slowly. "Now, these other wounds came afterwards."

"Afterwards?" I asked, knowing if someone had killed him then beat up the body postmortem, it was what I'd consider a hate crime.

Then we had a whole different amount of charges for the killer.

"Cracked ribs, right arm is broken in two places, along with a shattered femur. That's when the umbrella was shoved into him."

"Postmortem?" I made sure I was clearly understanding him.

"I wanted you to see this first, before I opened him and the DA or that snoopy lawyer tried to come back in here saying I cracked the ribs or broke any bones to perform the autopsy." He shoved a few of the photos he'd taken in my face. "I made sure I documented everything."

"We're looking for evidence of a hate crime." I glanced through the photos.

"Yeah. I believe so." He confirmed my suspicions. "And I don't think there was any sort of motive like robbery, because his watch and ring are still on. He's got a lot of cash in his wallet."

"A lot of cash?" I asked.

"At least a few thousand." Max caught me off guard. "I took photos of each one and sent them to your email."

"Thanks." My mind went into overdrive. "Wonder why he had so much cash?" I really wondered why Gary was working as a wedding waiter with thousands of dollars in his wallet. Seemed like something was off.

Max tucked his blue button-down shirt into his khaki pants before he turned to go back to his office. I followed him.

"Have a seat, and we can go over the preliminary again before I get started on the internal autopsy."

I sat down and looked around his pretty simple office.

He had a desk full of paper piled high, which I'd gotten used to seeing. On the wall were his medical license, business license, and coroner's license. He only had up the necessary items to prove who he was in case he was audited.

Max lived a simple life. He went to work, did his job, and enjoyed his home in the country. There wasn't any romance or social life that I knew of, but then again, I didn't stay in the gossip groups. He was able to keep his mouth completely zipped when it came to murder victims.

"The wife already called this morning to come identify the body." He looked at me as if he wanted me to clear it.

"That's fine. I need to talk to her. Maybe I'll wait around to question her." There was a buzz that rang on Max's computer.

He tapped the keyboard and looked at the screen.

"She's here now." He swiveled the monitor around to show me the video footage of her walking into the funeral home. He kept this system on his computer so when he was working alone, he knew when someone was coming in, since he couldn't hear anything from down in the basement.

She stood in the front room of the funeral home with her hands down to her sides and looked around.

"I'll go with you and leave after I ask her a few questions." I also wanted to understand why she'd not called Deputy Lee back.

Max and I didn't have much time to talk about anything else with Gary's X-ray, and I would wait until the internal autopsy was performed to ask any further questions.

For now, the X-ray told me enough about how Gary had died and that this was not just a little squabble. Someone had planned this. And it was my job to shift gears to see exactly what was in Mr. Futch's past to garner such an end to his life.

"Mrs. Futch." Max walked straight across the floor at the entrance of the funeral home. "I'm Max Bogus, the coroner, and this is Sheriff Lowry."

"I'm sorry to meet you under such circumstances." She didn't look at me when I addressed her.

"Why haven't you called Deputy Lee back?"

"After his initial visit to tell me about Gary, I needed a few hours to myself. It took everything I had to drag myself out of the house this afternoon to come here and..." Her voice fell away. Her eyes filled with tears.

Max stepped aside and plucked a few of the tissues from the box sitting on the credenza next to the wall, where there were flower arrangements and a few framed photos along with a condolence book for the corpse in the next room.

"You do know this is a murder investigation? And I'm going to need to ask you a few questions in order to find the person who did this to your husband and you." I wanted her to tell me that she'd answer some questions now, but she only continued to nod her head and look down at her feet.

"Mrs. Futch, do you understand what I'm asking of you?" I needed the confirmation.

"Brenda. Yes. I just can't think clearly right now." She swallowed, bringing her chin up. She had on a full face of makeup. Complete with lip liner and lipstick.

I'd never seen a woman who had just lost her husband in a tragedy with a full face of makeup on that hadn't run down her face. This was a concern and set off all sorts of alarms.

"Gary and I have been together for fifteen years. I can't imagine living life without him."

"Your husband had a large amount of cash on him. Do you know how he got that money?" I asked.

"No." She was quick to answer. A little too quick in my opinion.

"You have no idea why Gary would have thousands of dollars on him?" I tried to restate the question but was met with silence. "It's my understanding he was only making two hundred dollars for the entire night, and I'm not sure why Mr. Futch would want to do a job for such a little payout when he had the money in his pocket." I sucked in a deep breath when I noticed Poppa had joined us.

"Unless he was there for other reasons," Poppa said. "Follow the money."

For a split second I looked at Poppa then quickly followed up. "Unless he was there for other reasons," I repeated.

Both of us paused.

"Maybe he wanted to see someone from the wedding? Or someone invited to the wedding? There were a lot of government officials there. Did Gary have any dealings with anyone in the government?" I went on to theorize.

"No." She shook her head. "Not that I know of."

"What about anyone in the wedding party?" I asked. "Or the That's A Toast catering company he was working for."

"Working for?" The shock on her face told me she didn't have a clue where he was last night. "I don't know all the people Gary knows. He knows a lot of folks. He helps out a lot of people."

"Venetta Stenner, the owner of the company that employs your husband, said he'd been working for her for the past few months." I kept a close eye on her to gauge the response from her body. "Did you know that?"

She put her hand up. "I can't do this now."

"When can you do this?" I asked. "You see, I can't do my job and bring your husband's killer to justice until you give me some names of some people who might've wanted to do this to him."

"Maybe tomorrow." She turned to Max. "Can I please go see my husband now?"

Max glanced over at me.

I pinched a thin smile and nodded.

"I'm sorry for your loss," I told her as she walked past me to follow Max to the basement.

Poppa and I stood there in silence until we were alone.

"She's hiding something." Poppa took the words right out of my mouth.

"She sure is, but what?" I wondered.

CHAPTER THIRTEEN

"She had no idea her husband was doing the side gig." Poppa sat up in the front of the Wagoneer. "GGR513," Poppa repeated a few times.

"GGR513?" I asked as I pulled out of the parking lot of the funeral home.

"The license of the car Brenda was driving. I made sure I watched for her to come in so you could run the plates." Poppa was always so quick with all the details. "We need to run the plates and see if there's any stops."

"Great point." I picked up the phone to call Scott, since I didn't have my usual uniform with my walkie-talkie on it.

"Hey, Sheriff." Scott was always so professional.

"Can you run some plates for me and let me know if you come up with anything?" I asked him.

"Sure. Go ahead." I could hear some papers shuffling in the background.

I rattled off the license plate and told him to get back to me when he knew something before we hung up the phone.

"I have no idea. None of it makes sense. There was no employment history in his file Scott had pulled, so I wonder where their income comes from." I knew the little he was getting from the catering jobs wasn't enough for two people to live on. "I need to look into his wife. When I mentioned his job, she had a strange look on her face."

"Are you thinking she killed him?" Poppa took the words right out of my head.

"You and I both know we are to look at the spouse as the first person of interest, but when she wasn't at the wedding, I really thought it was Bradley." I knew it was all preliminary stuff, and weeding out suspects took time, but I wasn't one to dillydally. I liked to get things wrapped up pretty quickly. "Now we know Gary was hit in the head with something before someone did a number on his corpse."

"It would make sense if he was outside smoking and she was lurking in the darkness. When he was alone, she hit him from behind, grabbed the umbrella, and stabbed him with it." Poppa's theory could've easily been what had happened.

"And with little cooperation from her, or biding time, I. . ." I sighed and took a right on Broadway so I could go home and let Duke out. "I think I need to watch her for a little bit. Get a feel for what she's up to."

"I think you're right." Poppa rubbed his hands together in delight. "We are going on a stakeout."

"I reckon we are." I looked at him and smiled. "Even though we only get to see each other during these investigations, I do love being with you."

"What about that boy?" He referred to Finn.

"I love him, Poppa. I do, but. . ." My heart sank, taking my breath away.

"You can't have us both." Poppa told me something that made things so much more difficult for me.

"I don't want to be alone all of my life." I gripped the wheel. "Do you not like him because if I do spend the rest of my life with him, then you know you can't be here like you are now, or do you really not like him?"

There was a difference, and I needed to know why from Poppa.

"I don't want to leave you without protection. I don't know him well, and I know I can protect you. I can make sure you're okay in this job." He had such a strong voice and spoke with such conviction. "Being sheriff isn't the safest job in the world. You could be killed."

"Isn't that the risk you took all those years?" I asked and pulled into the driveway, shoving the gear shift into Park.

A horn beeped two quick times. Jolee's On the Run food truck pulled up to the curb in front of Mrs. Brown's house.

Poppa ghosted off. He left me with more questions than answers. My future with Finn wasn't what was most important right now. It was solving Gary's murder, and if I was going to get any answers about how elusive his wife had seemed, the only way was to do a little stakeout.

Duke was at the front window of the house. His nose prints had made smear marks all over the glass, and the window blinds were cockeyed.

"Hey, Jolee!" I called and waved. "I need to talk to you! Don't leave."

"Sounds good!" she called with the Styrofoam bowl of soup beans I'd gotten for her at church earlier today. She was doing her Sunday rounds for Meals on Wheels.

Jolee had a heart of gold. When she decided to open her food truck business, she had a mission to also give back. Meals on Wheels was a perfect volunteer job for her, and she had the perfect vehicle for it.

I heard Mrs. Brown greet Jolee when I walked around the side of my house so I could let Duke out into the backyard to burn off some energy.

"I'm sorry, buddy." I was greeted with the dancing dog at the back door. He jumped up a couple of times to say hello before he took off in a dead sprint, circling the yard a few times until he found the perfect scent, where he finally used the bathroom.

He darted back and forth a few times then dropped his ball at my feet. I threw it for him. Then he sauntered back up with his tongue hanging out of the side of his mouth.

"You're a good boy." I scratched his head a few times.

The gate rattled open.

"What's up?" Jolee came in the gate. Duke ran to the very back corner of the yard and quickly returned, dropping the ball he'd retrieved at Jolee's feet.

"Go get it!" She gave the ball a hard throw, sending it back to the corner.

"How many more deliveries do you have?" I asked.

"Mrs. Brown was the last one." Duke once again dropped the ball at her feet, and they started the fetch and throw game, doing this a few more times as we talked.

"Are you busy?" I asked.

"I was going to go home and sit outside, since it's so nice, with one of those masks I got at the Dixon's Foodtown while I read on my book-club book." She grinned. "You'd love it. It's a cozy mystery about a campground, and it's set in Kentucky."

Any books set in Kentucky were always enjoyable to read, since we lived here.

"It's a hoot. There's this group of ladies called the Laundry Club Ladies, and they solve crimes." The way she described it didn't sound like it was too different from life here in Cottonwood.

"I'll have to read it." It sounded interesting and fun. "I wonder if I can solve the murder in them?"

"I challenge you to read them. But other than that, I'm not doing much." She shrugged. "Not that Ben matters, but if we were dating, we'd be grilling out and going over the menus for the diner and my truck."

"I can do that while we stake out the victim's house."

"You mean like a real-life Laundry Club Ladies moment in the mystery I'm reading?" She lit up. A huge grin crossed her face.

"I guess, if that's something they do." I clicked my tongue a few times for Duke to come. "I think your food truck would be a good disguise."

"Sure. I'm all in. Now?" she asked and gave Duke a few pats down his back since he'd dropped himself on her feet.

"Now." I walked over to the door. "Come on, Duke. I'll give you some treats."

He jumped to his feet and darted into the open door.

"I'll be in the truck," Jolee called on her way out of the backyard. I heard the click of the gate, so I knew I didn't have to go out the back door to make sure it was locked.

"I promise we will go for a walk when I get home." Duke had followed me to the front door. He looked at me with sad hound-dog eyes that made my heart melt. "I said, I promise."

He sat down. There was a little hope in his eyes that I'd change my mind and take him, but I didn't. I grabbed my purse, phone, and keys and locked the front door behind me.

Jolee had already started the food truck.

"Where to?" she asked.

"They live on Liberty." I remembered reading Scott's report and trying to recall their house, but I'd not.

The food truck headed down Broadway toward Main Street, then Jolee took a left on Main. The way she gripped the wheel when we passed Ben's Diner made me decide to start talking because I could tell she was trying not to look.

Ben sure did break her heart, and that made me mad, but he was really a nice guy.

"What did you think of church today?" I asked.

"Really, Kenni, you don't need to save my feelings. You've never asked about church, and I know you're only trying to keep me from thinking about Ben." Jolee was one of the smartest people I knew.

"I don't like seeing you hurt. That's all." I looked out the window and watched us pass by the shops, making a plan in my head to go see Ruby and Viola tomorrow, now that I needed to make sure Mama didn't become the next suspect. "Are you going to the town council meeting tomorrow night?" We passed Cemetery Lane. It made me wonder where Poppa was.

"You know I am. I have to make sure no one tries to keep me from getting my monthly permits." She was talking about Ben yet again.

When she first started her food truck, she had to file permits in order to pull up and park to sell her food. Ben gave her one hell of a time. Anyone could protest her parking somewhere, but hopefully no one would.

"I'll be there. I think Bradley Ines is going to be there with his lawyer. She has a vendetta against me and my family because years ago, Poppa put her parents in jail, making her an orphan." I held on as she turned down Lake Street.

Soon we'd be on Liberty.

"She basically told me she had it in for me and would do anything to make sure I paid for putting her client in lockup without proper counsel." I knew it wouldn't fly in court if she did try to do something, but I always had to cover my back. "Now Mama has confessed just by opening her mouth that she'd borrowed the only piece of evidence I had tied to Bradley."

"The umbrella?" Jolee asked.

"How did you. . ." I started to say, but she didn't let me finish.

"Tibbie told me. She said that she didn't know how to tell you because your mom really did get on the waiter when he brought her a Long Island iced tea and not a sweet tea like she'd ordered. Then he told her she needed the Long Island because she was too wound up."

"He did?" Not that he wasn't right about Mama needing a little relaxation, but that he'd say something was out of character from what his wife and Venetta Stenner had said about his quiet and shy personality.

"That's what Tibbie said. She also said that your mama was outside the church waiting on Viola or somebody to go to the reception, and Bradley was walking out after the photos. He handed her the umbrella after Edna Easterly had gotten a wedding party photo of them in front of the church using the umbrellas." Again, something I wished Mama would've told me before I had gone all hog wild on Bradley.

I'd given her ample time to do such a thing when she was begging me to come back into the barn so I wouldn't get sick.

"Not that I think she did kill him, but it would explain why Bradley's umbrella was missing." Jolee slowly drove past the house. The car in the driveway looked like the same car I'd noticed in the funeral home parking lot, and it had the same plate I'd asked Scott to run for me.

"Go down and turn around. Park a few houses back." When I did a stakeout, I liked to be facing the main road so I could exit quickly. In this case, we'd be facing out toward Main Street.

"I'm sure you'll figure this out in no time. What's up with the wife?" Jolee put the truck in Park and climbed into the back of the truck.

I could hear her opening the refrigerator door, but I kept my eyes on the house.

"I'm not sure. She didn't really want to talk, but she did seem surprised when I told her he was working for the catering company. That's why I want to see what's going on over here." I sat up a little when I noticed a car had pulled up. A couple girls got out of the car before it zoomed off, but I couldn't get the license plate of that car.

Jolee got back up into the driver's seat with a couple of cans of Diet Coke for us and a bag of popcorn.

"We might as well snack on something." She set everything in the console attached to the front of the dashboard. She flipped on the radio. "Do you have any other suspects?"

It wasn't too long after that, maybe ten minutes, that I noticed another car had pulled up, and the same two girls ran out of the house and got into it before it zoomed off. This time I did get the license plate and texted it to Scott.

"The spouse, of course. Honestly, she wasn't even on my radar until the way she acted at the funeral home." Normally I didn't discuss cases with my friends, but Jolee was a good ear to lean on, and right now I was in an emotional turmoil with not only being threatened with being sued by the bride, but also by Bradley.

Add on the fact that Mama was pushing me down the aisle when I wasn't even engaged, plus trying to figure out what to do about Poppa and the dynamics of marrying Finn, if it ever did happen, was weighing heavily on me. Those issues made this whole murder thing seem like a cakewalk.

"She was very shocked, like I said, about her husband working for the catering service. And it is odd because we did find some money on him where it did raise a red flag about why he'd be doing the wedding.

Why was he at this wedding?" I asked and saw Brenda walk out of the house. "There's the wife."

"She doesn't look too upset to me," Jolee noticed.

"She sure doesn't, does she," I agreed. "Follow her," I instructed Jolee after Brenda had gotten into her car and pulled out.

Brenda didn't seem to notice us as she drove down to Main Street and hooked a left then an immediate right into the bank parking lot.

Jolee pulled the food truck up along the curb like she would on any given day, making it less obvious we were following Brenda in case she did notice us.

We watched as Brenda got out of the car and made a cash deposit in the ATM.

"Now what?" Jolee asked.

"Now I put going to bank to see Vernon Bishop with a warrant to see the finances of the Futches on my list." There was something tied to this money. I could feel it in my bones.

"Do you want me to keep following her?" Jolee asked.

"Nah." I needed to get back to the department so Scott and I could go over the clues we'd already collected as well as the game plan for the week. "Do you mind dropping me off at the department?"

"Not a bit." Jolee was able to drive the road parallel behind Main Street to avoid going back by the diner in fear of seeing Ben. She didn't say that, but I knew her well enough to know exactly how she would do anything to avoid seeing him.

"Let me know if you need something else." She smiled after she pulled up to the top of the alley, where she let me out.

"I know I don't have to say it, but I'm going to anyways." I held the door open and looked at her. "Don't tell anyone what we did today."

"I won't." She made a crisscross with her finger over her chest. "I'll call you tomorrow."

"Call me if you need me before that." By her reaction, I knew she was aware I was talking about Ben or just an ear. I shut the door and walked down the alley, eager to tell Scott what I'd just witnessed.

CHAPTER FOURTEEN

We used a big whiteboard on wheels with dry-erase markers. We could easily turn it around if someone came into the department. If we had a bigger department, I would've loved to have a room for investigating.

Scott had gotten a photo of Gary taped up on the board. There was one of Bradley and now Mama, both listed as suspects.

"I got all the photos from Edna's thumb drive." He stood at the whiteboard with the black marker in his hand as he scribbled names under them. He also had made bullet points under their names with the facts. Only the facts. "I also gave the guests at the wedding our email here to send in their photos. We already have a few, but I'm expecting a lot more."

"Make sure you get Polly Ryland's." I remembered her snapping a lot at the wedding when she wanted me to move my big head out of the way, plus I'd seen her gushing over all the decorations at the reception, the phone never leaving her hand.

I stood back and watched while he finished writing what we knew. At some point during the investigation, all of this would make sense.

"I have a list of guests printed out in the file." Scott was so good at taking his instructions and following through without me even having to ask him a second time.

"We need to add Brenda Futch to the list." I gave Scott a brief rundown about what Jolee and I had witnessed, before I called the judge to ask for a warrant for the financial records for the Futches.

Judge agreed I had enough evidence with the money alone to get the warrant, and he'd fax it over to me by morning.

"Where did you put the thumb drive from Edna?" I asked him.

"I downloaded them onto our hard drive, so you should be able to pull them up." He looked at his watch.

"Great." I walked over to my desk and sat down, wiggling the keyboard mouse so my computer monitor would come to life. "I'm going to take my time this afternoon to go through them. All of them. Wow."

There were more than a thousand photos.

"There's a lot of them too." Edna Easterly must've taken a photo of every single detail of this wedding. "You go on home. You've worked way too much this weekend, and I'm sure you've got something or someone to go home to."

"Are you sure?" he asked, eluding my hopes of him divulging any information about the mention of someone.

"Of course. Get out of here." I waved to the door. "You need to take some time before we really hit it hard this week. I'm hoping to find some photos in here of anyone near Mama when she was having her little tizzy. As well as all the movements of the waiter."

The good thing about Edna's photos and being so many, I could tell from the initial few I'd looked at so far that there was almost an exact timeline of events.

Scott headed out, leaving me alone with the photos and the whiteboard. There had to be something in them, and really I didn't have much to do over the next couple of hours. Duke would be fine at home.

Edna had gotten Jasmine before the wedding, sitting with the bridesmaids, to a private moment with Jasmine and her father. If I clicked fast enough through them, it was like a reel in a movie.

Click, click, click.

The movement of my finger pushing down the mouse button was the only sound piercing my ears.

One after the other was white tulle, bright teeth, and huge smiles all around.

Until.

Edna's photos of the groomsmen in their room where they were getting ready.

They appeared to be pretty normal—pats on the back for Dickie, the passing of the bourbon bottle where they were all either taking a gulp or filling up a flask, to the endearing one of Bradley handing the ring box to Dickie, and the usual one where they were all posing.

Nothing here that caught my eye as I clicked on through.

Click, click, click.

One after the other, the photos scrolled. Each time Bradley caught my eye, I'd pause for a moment and search the surroundings to see if anything jumped out.

Then it did.

Jasmine and Dickie had gotten their wedding photos taken before the bride walked down the aisle. From an arm's length, one of the photos appeared as the rest. Everyone facing forward, the bride and groom in the middle while the wedding party stood on each side. Groomsmen on one side, bridesmaids on the other.

Until.

I clicked the mouse to zoom in, and in one particular photo, Bradley's eyes were shifted to the right as though he were focusing on Jasmine.

The pose changed to where the groomsmen were surrounding Jasmine, and there was an ever-so-slight touch from Bradley that would've gone unnoticed by anyone else. Edna had used a rapid-fire shutter speed during the event, and unless someone had their eye on Bradley, you'd never have seen his subtle and quick gentle touch on her arm, where she slowly eased it away and glared at him.

"Do you think they were having an affair?" Poppa had ghosted himself over my shoulder.

"I don't know. I do know Bradley is certainly not over her after all of these years. What is that song with Garth Brooks about showing up at the wedding to toast the bride and groom?" I asked, trying to recall how it went exactly, though it didn't matter. "For some reason it's escaping me."

"I don't listen to all that new country stuff." Poppa snarled. "Give me some Hank Williams and some Patsy Cline, then we can compare."

Poppa drifted off into some twangy, sad song while I clicked and clicked rapidly to when the bridal party had come to the reception.

"They played the song." Thank goodness Edna was click happy with the camera, because she got the sequence of photos that I recalled from when the bridal party came into the reception and he sang the song so loud before the waiter walked by with the shot glasses.

"He took two." I had thought I'd seen him just do one shot. "Look at the waiter."

"What?" Poppa stopped belting out the music. He gave his attention to the screen.

"The song was playing when the bridal party had come to the reception. Bradley didn't miss a note. He waltzed in and started singing just as the waiter passed, like it was rehearsed this way. It was flawless." I clicked through the sequence of photos to show Poppa a few times before I zoomed in on Gary's face, where there was really more of an amused look.

It was Bradley's face that stopped me in my tracks.

"Have you ever stood at the intersection of a crosswalk and thought the coast was clear to walk. You take the first step off the curve, and a car zooms by, sending you into a heart attack?" I asked Poppa and blew up Bradley's face when he really took a moment to look at the waiter. "That initial wave of shock and feeling when you almost got hit and killed?"

"Yeah." Poppa was trying to figure out where I was going with this.

"That's the look on Bradley's face when he did finally look into

Gary's eyes." I pointed to Bradley. "But not Gary. He has a very satisfied look on his face. As if taking pleasure in Bradley noticing him."

"They know each other." Poppa slid his ghostly glance to me. "Good work, Kenni bug. Good work."

When I printed the photos off, I made sure I did it one at time, processing them in order by writing the order on the back of the photo. I'd even blown them up so you could clearly see the facial expressions on both. Once I had what I felt was some sort of interaction that warranted another conversation with Bradley, I taped them up on the whiteboard and took a couple of steps back to gain some perspective.

As clear as day, there was true recognition of the other.

I picked up the file and opened it, laying it flat on my desk. I used my finger to scan down the page until I found Janice's phone number. Right next to it was Bradley's.

"Bradley." I was a bit shocked he'd answered. I'd decided to call him first and if he hesitated then call Janice. "I have a few photos at the station that I would like you to look at. Do you think you could call Janice and see if the two of you could come down here really fast so we can get this cleared up and your name out of it?"

"If that's the case, I don't need her." He was giving up his right to counsel.

I had to make it very clear he was doing so.

"You are being recorded," I quickly murmured and hit the record button. "It's my understanding that you are giving up your right to have counsel present while you are going to come down here and look at photos taken from the wedding reception of Jasmine and Dickie Dee?"

"Yes. If it's just photos I need to ID. Do you know how much Janice is costing me?" He laughed.

"I'm sorry. I do not, but I'm here, so if you'd like to come down here and take a look, or you can call Janice to meet you here as your counsel." I stated it again for the record.

"Nah." He played it off, not realizing what I was about to hit him with. "I can come on down. I was about to leave town, anyways. I can do it on my way out."

"Leave town?" I asked.

"Yeah. The wedding party is continuing the fun by going on a group honeymoon."

My heart stopped.

I was not sure if he said goodbye first or I did, because he threw me for a big loop.

"Judge, it's Sheriff Lowry." I knew I had to talk fast. "It's my understanding the bride and groom from the murder investigation are taking the entire wedding party on their honeymoon, and they are leaving tonight. I can't let that happen. We've yet to have time to interview the participants as well as the guests."

"Yes. Yes, sir." I listened to the judge clarify what I was asking him to do as he talked from the other end of the line. "Yes. I need you to make sure they stay in Cottonwood until I can get all of their statements."

"Well, sir, we are a bit shorthanded tonight. Seeing how it's just me and a Sunday." He was trying to talk me into having the twelve come down tonight to give their statements. "Yes, sir. Yes, sir. Fine."

I eased the phone back down on the cradle.

"You didn't win that one, did you?" Poppa asked.

"Nope. He is going to call the district attorney and have her call Jasmine and Dickie to let them know they can't leave town until they give their statements. Which will be tonight." I hesitated even though I knew I needed to call Betty Murphy and Scott Lee to come in.

Neither of them protested too much, but there was a lot of hemming and hawing on Betty's part.

Before too long, the door of the department flew open.

Jasmine Dee had her hands fisted at her sides with the look of the devil on her face as she glared at me, gritted her teeth, and bolted into the department with her daddy and Janice by her side.

CHAPTER FIFTEEN

"This is ridiculous." Jasmine started to throw down before Janice stepped in front of her.

Jasmine's head bobbled to and fro trying to get a look at me.

"Here we go again." Scott sighed and gestured for one of the bridesmaids to come sit down at his desk.

"I will be filing a lawsuit against you and the city of Cottonwood tomorrow while my clients are on their way to their honeymoon. Now you've ruined this for them. We will be seeking damages for not only the cost of the reception venue since they weren't able to get back their money from the caterer or the venue." Her lung capacity was amazing. She didn't stop to take a breath. "This lawsuit will also be introduced at the town council meeting tomorrow night so they are well aware of the taxpayer dollars their sheriff is using up over some ridiculous theory in her head that is based on her own mind instead of evidence. Or how she's trying to cover up her own mother's wrongdoing."

"You get her, Kenni!" Poppa danced on his feet. "Don't you let her talk about your mama like that."

"The quicker you stop talking, the faster we can get these people out of here." I didn't show any emotion as I stared back into Janice's eyes. There was no fear where I stood. "I am the sheriff. This is how I run an investigation in my town, and if I let any one of these witnesses leave town before I can get a statement, it would be negligent of my duties the citizens have elected me to do." I pushed past her, grabbed some statement sheets off the edge of Scott's desk, and called my biggest concern. "Bradley Ines."

"Oh no. I think we've already talked to Bradley," Janice protested, coming between me and Bradley.

"Bradley and I have already discussed the reason I need to talk to him again." I picked up the file and opened it, taking out the extra photos I'd run off before he'd gotten there since I'd already turned the whiteboard around so no one could see the timeline I'd created with them.

After I handed the photos to her, she quickly thumbed through them.

"I'm going to need time to talk to my client before I let him answer any questions you have to say regarding photos." Janice looked at Bradley and gave a slow shake of her head. "I'm sorry, but you may not talk to him at this time."

"So what?" Bradley scoffed and shrugged at her. "I don't get to go on the trip?"

"I'm sorry. No. I can't take care of you and all of them before the flight leaves in the morning. You're going to have to go later in the week." There was a little more discussion between the two of them, and I excused myself for a brief moment when the door opened and Mama was standing there, gawking in.

"Mama." I took her outside. "What are you doing here?" I asked.

"What are all of them doing here?" she questioned me back.

"You shouldn't be here," I told her and ushered her back to her car. "Is that Viola?" I glanced up when I noticed Viola walking around the alley.

"Mmhmm." Mama's brows pinched. "She told me something was going on, and I was left a little uneasy after I felt like that woman in there accused me of killing the waiter, so I decided to come on back down here, because I've been thinking about this."

"We've been thinking about this." Viola pointed between the two of them.

Oh boy. It was awful when Mama got to thinking about something, but with the two of them thinking, it was a travesty. Nothing good.

"What are you two up to?" I asked before I plugged my fingers in my ears. "Don't tell me. I don't want to know." I burrowed my fingers deeper. "Lallallaaa," I sang out when I noticed Mama and Viola's lips were moving at the same time.

Mama grabbed my forearm and tugged it down.

"Fine. Me and Viola will do our own snooping," Mama warned. "Come on, Viola. Let's go get a sweet tea from Ben's Diner."

A few hours later, I was sitting in the chair on my back porch. I was exhausted from all of the statements and just the entire day's activities. There was nothing more discovered about the murder than when I had woken up.

Poppa had disappeared, and Duke was pouting because I'd left him alone all day even though I'd given him almost an entire box of treats.

"Knock, knock." Finn had come through the gate, and I'd not even heard him. "Goodness, you must be tired if you didn't hear me come in."

"I'm mentally spent from Mama and Janice," I told him and took my feet out of the seat of the empty chair. It scooted a little away from me when I gave it a little shove so Finn could sit down with me. "Mama and Viola are up to something, but it'll die down, because they were so excited to tell me about their grand plan but then gave up literally one minute into trying to get me to listen."

"Do you want to talk it out?" he asked.

"You have your own crimes to deal with." I sat up and rested my elbows on my thighs, leaning forward into him. "Unless you want to come back and work at the sheriff's department. I'm happy to make room."

"You are doing great. Don't let that lawyer get to you. Her parents must've been pretty bad if they were both convicted." Finn kissed the tip of my nose. "What do you have so far?"

He really did know all the facts already, but going over everything—

how Gary was knocked in the head, giving him the fatal blow, and the umbrella made it a hate crime—once more with him did start to make a picture in my head.

"I have these photos from Edna's camera, and you can see Gary and Bradley recognize each other. There's a connection, but I'm not sure what." I sighed and stood up, since I knew it was getting close to bedtime and I needed some sleep. "I think I'm going to go back to visit Gary's wife tomorrow and show her the photo. Maybe she'll recognize Bradley."

"Good idea." He got up and stood in front of me, holding both of my hands down to his side. "You keep doing you. You are a wonderful sheriff, and you're smart. You have a great sense of intuition, and if you feel this is the lead you need to take, then that's the lead."

"I sure do miss you in the department. Seeing you every day and getting these little pep talks are nice." I rolled up on my toes and kissed him.

"You know I'm here for you." There was a tone in Finn's voice that I'd never heard from him, but I sure had heard that same tone with my daddy when he talked Mama down from something.

My gut clenched.

Was Finn thinking about proposing? Was Mama's dream finally going to come true?

He was right about one thing. I had a very good intuition.

CHAPTER SIXTEEN

"Kenni, Kenni." I heard my mama calling me. My eyes opened. It was five a.m.

I groaned and pulled the covers over my head, knowing I'd been dreaming or having a nightmare about Mama.

"Kendrick Lowry, you get out of that bed right now!"

My eyes popped open. I threw back the sheet and bolted to an upright position.

"Mama." I grasped the edges of the covers when I saw her standing at the bedroom door and pulled them up to my chin as Viola White's eyeballs looked over Mama's shoulder into my bedroom. "I guess it wasn't a dream."

"We have no time to talk about your dreams. Now get up and get your clothes on," she insisted. "Me and Viola have got some news about this here murder. It proves I didn't kill no one."

"Slow down, Mama," I told her. "Why don't you and Viola go get a pot of coffee on while I get some appropriate clothing on. Then we can talk about what it is you're all in a tizzy about at five a.m."

My voice did stress the time so she'd get the point.

"I already let Duke out and fed him." She turned. "Come on, Viola. Let Kenni have her privacy."

Privacy.

That was one word Mama didn't understand the meaning of. Especially when it came to me. Daddy told me not to give Mama the extra key to my house after I'd moved in and had the locks changed. He said she'd be over here all the time, letting herself in. She sure did.

But so did Daddy. If he knew Duke was home all by himself, Daddy would come over and get Duke, take him to their house, and let him be spoiled all day.

Now, I couldn't entirely believe it was Daddy's idea because every time Duke did visit, Mama always had something delicious on the table and insisted she had no idea Daddy was bringing Duke home. Which meant I had to pick Duke up, in turn making me stop by their house. Then have supper, which was always a four-course, Southern-style meal accompanied by an after-supper drink.

"Must be nice to still be able to sleep in while we are out there solving the murder," Viola's under-breath grumble was really meant for me to hear her.

"Ohhhhhh." I gave myself one of those long sighs to prepare myself for whatever it was they'd decided to look into. "At least they aren't dead," I told myself as I peeled back the warm covers and put my feet on the floor.

Instead of throwing something on just to go see what they'd stirred up, I decided to get dressed. Viola was right about one thing—there was still a murder to be solved.

There was no way I was going to go back to bed, so I went straight to my closet and grabbed one of my clean sheriff uniforms. The brown outfit did nothing for my looks, but at least it was something I didn't have to think too hard about putting on, like most people when they went to work. That part of it didn't make me mind wearing the same outfit day in and day out.

I strapped on my utility belt because I knew if I carried it out into the kitchen, Mama would've been all touchy-feely over it, and then one of us might've been dead.

I padded down the hall and heard whispering between them, as much as two older women can whisper.

"I think she'll be fine." Mama was confident in her words.

"I don't. She ain't gonna like us lying to her." Viola really got my attention, but they stopped talking when they heard me, so I took a left into my only bathroom.

"I'm going to brush my teeth and wash my face," I called down to them and barely shut the door once I was inside. I kept my ear open.

"Do you reckon they saw us?" Viola asked.

"If they did, they don't know me or you." Mama again was adamant about something to where Viola was not convinced.

"That's a lie, Vivian Lowry, if I ever heard one," Viola protested. "You told me you thanked him for the umbrella, and trust me, his lawyer, that woman, has probably learned everything about you she can because she's gonna be at the town council meeting tonight. They are going to announce the lawsuit against the sheriff's department, Kenni, and the county."

"That only means Kenni has today to look into things to prove I'm innocent, and me and you just got the evidence we needed."

"Lordy be." I jerked open the bathroom door and bolted down the hallway. "What on earth did you two do?"

"We, um. . . we, um. . ." Viola shuddered, pushing her fingers in her gray hair. A sure sign of nervousness.

"Go on, tell her." Mama's hand whacked Viola's arm. "You're the reason we are here, and you've been dying to tell her."

"You tell her. You said she would be upset." Viola's eyes dropped to my gun. "And with that gun on her, she looks a little scary."

"Viola, you've seen me with my belt on a million times." I sucked in a deep breath, my eyes shifting between the two. "What is it you two did?"

"Don't you need to fix your hair?" Mama's brows furrowed.

"What. Did. You. Two." I wagged my finger between them. Duke was scratching at the door. "Do?"

"Duke wants in." Mama was trying to waste time.

"He can wait."

"Fine. Last night when you caught us in the alley behind the department. . ." Mama gulped.

"Go on." I gave a hard head nod.

"We put a tracker on Bradley Ines's car."

My jaw dropped. That was the last thing I'd ever think Mama would do.

"Viola saw it on a television show, and we ordered one. Did you know you can get packages next day from the internet?" Mama looked as pleased as a dog with two tails.

"You did what?" I still hadn't gotten past the initial shock of the two of them buying a tracker.

"It was really easy like." Viola nodded, shaking the large turquoise beads that lay in three strands around her neck. She looked like she was about to have a fancy photo shoot with all her makeup on, hair styled, and full of jewelry. "You have to sync it to your phone, which Toots Buford knew exactly how to do when I took it down to Tiny Tina's."

"Yep. You just pull the sticky thing off and pop it up underneath the car, anywhere." Mama talked like they were experts. "And you pull up that little app thingy Toots put on my phone, and it showed this little car going on the road."

"Show her, Viv," Viola encouraged Mama.

"No." I put my hand up. "I don't want to have any more information. Do you understand what Viola just said about Janice suing me? Now you are an accomplice to a suspect." I pointed directly at Viola.

"No. I don't. No. I. . ." Viola had lost her words. "I was being a friend to Viv. If that's a crime"—she threw her wrists out in front of her, making the bangles jingle-jangle—"arrest me."

I unclipped my cuffs off my utility belt.

"If you insist." I walked over.

"Kendrick Lowry!" Mama hollered. "I'd be ashamed. You don't even know what we found out when we tracked him."

"I don't want to know."

"You would if you knew it was the victim's house. Where he was in there for at least an hour." Mama did have some interesting information.

"Go on." I put my cuffs back on my utility belt.

Duke had given up on the door. He was either running around the yard or had decided to lie by the door.

"That's right. We tracked him straight over to Gary Futch's house." Viola crossed her arms. "I think we got us a connection. I said Bradley and Mrs. Futch are having an affair, and they got rid of the husband. I saw the same thing on my crime show."

Not half bad, though I didn't tell them that.

"Did they see you?" My mind came up with a few ways I was going to need to spin this so Mama didn't go to jail for obstruction of justice, not to mention how I wasn't able to keep my own mother in check.

"No." Viola shook her head. "We made sure they didn't, but I can't tell you how shocked we were."

Mama nodded her head slowly.

"They were more than a suspect who might've killed that woman's husband. They were in there for a while. Do you understand what I'm saying?" Mama asked, eyes wide open.

"They didn't see you?" I needed to ask one more time.

"Not me." Mama's chin slid to the right, her eyes looked up toward the ceiling, and her lips pursed. She tried hard not to look at me.

"You?" I turned to Viola.

"I was only trying to make sure the tracker stayed in place because he was driving like a bat out of hell and hit the curb." Viola had me for a loss of words. "What? He hit the curb, and it could've fallen off."

"Did he see you?" I asked again since it was clearly the only answer I cared about.

"It's hard tellin'." She sighed. The coffeepot beeped. "Oh good. Coffee."

"Did anyone see her?" I asked Mama. "You better tell me now, because if you don't and someone springs it on me, I won't be able to protect you or me. Do you realize you've not only put yourself in jeopardy, but also Viola and me?"

"It was Viola's idea." Mama was quick to call her out.

"I mentioned how I saw someone on the television," Viola spoke up.

"It's the semantics." Mama used her favorite word to get herself out of a sticky situation and used the task of getting us all a coffee to avoid looking at me.

"I don't need to know any more." I put my hands up. "The less I know, the better."

"This can't be all bad, Kenni bug." I looked up at the door and saw Poppa standing on the other side.

I walked over to the screen door and popped it open.

"What on earth is wrong with that dog?" Viola had leaned over from the kitchen chair far enough to see out.

Mama grabbed a tea towel out the drawer and swiped the countertop on her way over to take a gander at Duke. Poppa must've been keeping Duke quiet and content while I was inside questioning Mama and Viola.

"Viola, you forget he's a very important poo-leece dog. My granddog." Mama clicked her tongue.

"Go," Poppa demanded with a snap of his finger.

Woof! Duke barked and darted into the house.

"See?" Mama grinned like a possum. "He loves his granny."

"Mmhhhmmm," I hummed and stepped out of the way of the door so Poppa could enter as a living being would, but he didn't. I sighed and shut the door. "Back to this little tracker situation."

I wanted to bring Poppa into the conversation because I knew he was able to think a little clearer than me, since I was trying to weed through all the hemming and hawing Mama and Viola had going on between them. Each was pointing the finger at the other.

"Let's go back to the theory of the affair." Poppa's ghost stood in the corner.

"You mentioned Brenda and Bradley might be an item." I picked up the cup of coffee, walked over to the table, and sat down.

Mama was digging through the refrigerator freezer.

"Where is your coffee cake?" Mama asked, her head stuck all the way in.

"I don't keep coffee cake, Mama." I knew this was going to open a can of worms—I just didn't realize it was going to be a bucket of them.

Viola White let out a gasp. Mama's face contorted.

"This is why you aren't married. Don't you understand people want to feel welcome when they pop over?"

"Mama! I'm not married because I don't want to be married!" There was a knock on the screen door. "I don't want to get married. Do you understand?" I said on the way over to the door.

"I understand." Finn stood on the other side of the screen.

CHAPTER SEVENTEEN

"They are infuriating," I seethed on the phone with Finn after I got Mama and Viola out of the house, so I could go back to Brenda Futch's to check out exactly why Bradley Ines had gone there this morning.

I rubbed my neck. There was a sudden pain. I couldn't help but wonder if I'd gotten whiplash from watching Finn dart out so fast. Had he heard me say I wasn't getting married?

"You scared that boy off." Poppa's voice carried from the back seat because Duke was standing on the passenger side seat of the Wagoneer with his head stuck out of the window. His ears flapped back from the wind, his tongue was out, and his tail beat a rhythm on the seat back, showing his heart's happiness.

"I had no intentions of doing so." I tried not to think too much about why Finn had run off so fast, but it didn't take a big college degree to figure it out. "I only wanted Mama to see what her and Viola had done to compromise the investigation."

"Kenni bug, your mama and I only want what's best for you." Poppa was playing both sides of the fence.

"You and Mama are on opposite teams." I glanced in the rearview mirror so I could look at Poppa's ghost. "She wants me to marry Finn.

You want me to break up with Finn. Either way I'm losing." I gripped the wheel at the stop sign at the end of Free Row and took a left on Main Street.

It was too early to go check out Mama's story at Brenda's house and too late in the morning to sneak over to the Tattered Cover Books and Inn, where Bradley was staying while in town, to get the tracker, which I had planned on doing.

It was best to go to the department and check in with Betty and Scott before I got started on the full day of investigating.

I had to find something to take to the town council meeting. I wasn't sure what, but going to Tiny Tina's was definitely in the schedule, as well as going to Dixon's Foodtown to talk to Toots Buford.

"If I don't get married, Mama is going to die because she thinks I'll be labeled an old spinster. If I do get married, I can't have you." My eyes stung. My nose flared as I tried to keep the emotional feeling of never seeing Poppa again deep inside, buried where it'd been for years before his ghost appeared. "I've lived without you before, and it wasn't easy. But I love Finn too. I can't deny him a life where he could be happily married and with children."

"Are you telling me you've got that mothering instinct?" Poppa smiled.

"Goodness, I don't know, but I do know Finn is really good with kids." Memories of Finn and me working as a team here in the sheriff's department for a few years before he became sheriff in Clay's Ferry flooded my mind. "Life in Cottonwood isn't murder all the time. We did some fun things together, like hand out the cute sticker sheriff's badges to the kids at all the events. Finn was really good with the kids. So much better than me."

"You would be a fine mother." Poppa's thick and wiry brows knotted. "I guess it's not fair of me to continue to ask you not to be with him. He is a good man, Kenni bug. I know he'd protect and care for you. Provide a good life."

"What are you saying?" I asked and looked in the rearview mirror. He wasn't there. I twisted around to see in the back seat. He was gone.

Beep, beep.

A horn called out from behind the Jeep.

My eyes shifted to the side mirror where someone had stopped at the stop sign behind me, signaling me to go.

I threw my hand in the air and hit the gas, pulling out on Main Street, but not without the feeling Poppa had something drastic he was going to do. Not with me. Not with my relationship with Finn.

But him.

"What's wrong with you?" Betty Murphy sat at her desk across from me with narrowed eyes. "You ain't right today."

"I'm thinking about this case." I had settled down in front of my computer once Duke and I got to the station. Duke was content with the treat Betty had given him and he'd lain down in the dog bed next to my desk, on his back, legs in the air.

"That's not thinking about a case." Betty was quick to point out. "I've sat here looking at you for years now, and that's not a look I've ever seen during an investigation. You go from this." She made a very still face. "To this." She grinned. "Then to this." She frowned.

She nailed every single emotion I was feeling with the thoughts of Mama, Finn, and Poppa in my head that traveled to my heart. I loved each of them so dearly, I couldn't disappoint one of them without affecting the other.

"You can tell me what's wrong." Betty's eyes softened. She was so mothering, and I loved that about her, even though we were in a working environment.

Scott had yet to get to the department, which left plenty of room for me to talk to Betty, but there was nothing she could really do since, well... Poppa.

Could you imagine the look on Betty's face when I told her my poppa was a ghost, not to mention a ghost deputy who only appeared when there was a murder in Cottonwood? Or the fact that I had to choose a life with him in it and Finn not? Why, she'd report me to the loony bin in a split second.

I decided to keep my mouth shut and lie.

"I am thinking about Jasmine and Dickie Dee. When Gary's body appeared, I immediately went into sheriff mode." Technically this wasn't a lie. It was the truth, but not what she was asking about. "I didn't take into consideration their feelings about me ruining their big day."

"No, you didn't!" Mayor Chance Ryland stood at the door between Cowboy's Catfish and the department.

Mayor Ryland was debonair and fit for a man in his sixties. His black hair was slicked back, his strong jaw tensed. He'd started running, dying his hair black, and growing the goatee along with doing a lot of manscaping after he'd started dating Polly Parker, who was now the First Lady of Cottonwood.

"Do we have to do this now?" Polly had walked in behind him. "I'm going to be late for my nail appointment."

Polly looked at her petite hands. The diamond rings on her fingers clicked against each other as she picked her cuticles.

She looked up at me with her big puppy-dog eyes. Her perfectly lined pink pouty mouth contorted, her nose snarled, and she spat between the veneers I was sure were stuck in her small mouth.

"He's been throwing a dying duck fit to come in here and talk to you, but I told him to let it be." She moved her hands down to her belly. Slowly she rubbed it counterclockwise. "I told him to watch his stress at his age. After all, we've got a little bundle of joy coming into this world who needs her daddy."

"You're pregnant?" That was the last news I'd expected to hear. Especially after I'd thought men of a certain age weren't able to have children, much less one of Mayor Ryland's age. The age of Polly's own daddy.

"Yes." Polly squealed like a pig. All of her five-foot-two-inch, one-hundred-pound frame bounced on her toes with delight. "We are going to be parents."

"What, are you going to be, like, ninety when that kid graduates from preschool?" Betty Murphy slammed her lips together. Obviously she hadn't kept in her private thoughts as she'd hoped.

"Betty Murphy!" Polly shrieked in horror. "I told you. I told you we'd be made fun of."

Polly twirled around and darted back into the restaurant.

"We are going to have a talk about this lawsuit later today." He gave me and Betty a hard look before he turned to go after his wife. "Honey. She's an old woman. Old women have no filter," we heard him saying.

"Am I wrong?" Betty asked me with a straight face, before we both started to laugh so hard we didn't even hear Scott come in the department door.

"I must've missed something really good." He dropped a piece of paper on my desk.

I picked it up and looked at it.

"The warrant for the bank." I smiled. "Good work, Deputy Lee." I had my first stop of the day. "Before I go, we need to talk about something I found out today."

"What's that?" he asked.

"I can't tell you how or who told me yet." I knew I had to keep Mama and Viola's little stakeout under wraps. "I've got two witnesses who aren't ready yet to come forward with information, but they swear they saw Bradley Ines visiting Brenda Futch's house."

I stood up and walked over to the whiteboard. I gripped one side and pushed it back to face the room.

I picked up the dry-erase marker and popped the lid off so I could write. I drew an arrow from Brenda's photo to Bradley's photo.

"These two know each other." I dotted the end of the marker on the board next to each one of their names. "I'm not sure in what capacity. I only know their visit wasn't just a friendly one. It just so happens he was there for a while, and let's just say they didn't end the visit by screaming."

"Do you mean they were more than friendly?" Betty asked.

"There wasn't any physical activity, if that's what you mean, seen by the two witnesses."

"Two witnesses?" Scott asked.

"Alright. It was Mama and Viola. Viola had come up with this big, grand scheme she's seen on one of those crime shows."

"Those shows are going to be the death of law enforcement." Betty shook her head. "People just think they can do what they show on television."

Who was Betty trying to kid? She was the biggest gossip in all of Cottonwood, and normally she was the one who broadcast what was going on with cases better than any news station.

"Anyways, they put a tracker on his car when he was here yesterday with Janice. They tracked him, and he went to the Futches' house. After I go to the bank to see exactly what was going on with all the money in Gary's pocket and his finances, I'm going to go straight over to see Bradley and find out why he went over to the victim's house." I had a solid plan and hoped for some good answers to present to the town council tonight.

Not that what the town council said or thought mattered. It didn't. They couldn't fire me, and I wasn't quitting, but the townsfolk sure could fire me at the next election if I didn't have some sort of news to report in my defense, since I knew Janice was going to present her case tonight as if we were in a court of law. She'd use the townsfolk as the jury, and I wasn't ready to be tried for a case I'd yet to solve or even gotten a good handle on the suspects.

Plus if I didn't come up with something for Mama, because I knew it was where Janice would go, she'd present at the council meeting that I was going after her client so Mama wouldn't be a suspect, and that was not true.

"Now that I have the warrant for the bank and the Futches' accounts, I'll be able to see if there's some sort of money trail tied to Gary and why he'd have so much cash in his possession at the time of death."

Something deep in my bones told me to follow the money, besides Poppa's whispers here and there.

"I'm telling you to follow the money." Poppa appeared next to the whiteboard.

"Do you want me to go to the bank so you can pay a visit to Bradley?" Scott asked. "Or I can go see Bradley."

"No." I went back to my computer and hit a few keys to bring up my email. "I want you to go through some of these photographs sent in by some of the wedding guests. I hope we can see some action shots with something in the background with any sort of evidence."

"Sounds good." Scott came over to my desk and sat down. "I'll let you know if I see something."

"What can I do?" Betty asked.

"Just man the phones and make sure everyone else in Cottonwood is all good." I didn't anticipate any sorts of calls coming in that she and Scott couldn't take care of. "I'll let you two know if I find out anything at the bank."

I gave a couple of clicks to my tongue.

Duke jumped to his feet and trotted to the door with me.

Cottonwood First National Bank was literally a block down the road. Since I wasn't really sure what we were about to find out with the warrant, I'd decided to drive. If I did find something out that had to do with driving somewhere, I didn't want to waste what daylight hours I had left before the town council meeting by walking to the department to fetch the Jeep.

It was easiest to drive.

The parking lot was empty, which was to be expected since I arrived right as they'd opened. The teller line was along the back wall, and the offices were in the front behind glass walls. There was literally no privacy for Vernon Bishop, so when our eyes caught, he couldn't run from me.

He waved me in and stood up.

He wore a nice three-piece black pinstripe suit. His hair, which was prematurely gray, was neatly combed to the side with the perfect amount of gel. His cologne was a nice touch. He was much younger than he looked—fifteen years older than me, to be exact.

"Sheriff, it's awfully early for you to do some banking business," he greeted me. His eyes shifted to the piece of paper in my hand. "I'm guessing this is about Gary Futch?"

"It sure is." I put the warrant on his desk and slid it across.

"Have a seat." He gestured, sitting himself, and picked up the paper. "This is for Mr. Futch."

"It sure is. We found thousands of dollars in his pocket at the scene of the crime. He was working for two hundred dollars, and well, I just can't seem to wrap my head around why he'd want to cater an event for two hundred dollars when he had thousands. Which makes me think he was either in debt and trying to make as much money as he could to pay something off, or he was at the wedding for some other reason. There's no better place to start than his banking needs."

"I'd love to help you, but Mr. Futch doesn't have an account here."

"What about Brenda Futch?" I asked.

"This warrant is for a Gary Futch." Vernon had me, and he wasn't budging. He put the piece of paper back on the desk and slid it back across to me. "Now, if you had a different warrant, I might be able to help you."

"Vernon." My head tilted. "You and I both know that I'm going to come back here with another warrant, so you might as well save us time and just give the sheriff's department what I need."

"I'm sorry. I can't do that without a warrant, because I'm not a mind reader. I can't tell what you're thinking or who you need what for." Vernon wasn't stupid. He knew good and well what I was there for.

"Fine. Then can you tell me if there's anything illegal going on?" I asked in case there wasn't any need to get a warrant for Brenda. "Anything that might be of help to the investigation into the death of Gary Futch?"

"Brenda is a businesswoman. She's got a good business for one of the oldest professions for women." He shrugged.

"Is she a Mary Kay consultant?" I wondered, recalling all the makeup on her face.

"I can't answer that, but she does make good money for women." He was talking in signals.

"I'll be back." I didn't have time for charades and decided to just call in the warrant to the judge in hopes it'd be sent into the department by the time I got back from my little visit with Bradley Ines.

This time I didn't bother driving the Jeep. Instead, Duke and I walked down to the inn, since it was located in the block between the department and the bank. Plus it was next to Ben's Diner. Not that I needed more on my plate, but Jolee was my best friend, and stopping in to get a biscuit and gravy along with a cup of coffee was the icebreaker I needed to pick Ben's brain about why he was being a jerk to Jolee.

Duke followed alongside of me. I texted Finn as we walked on the sidewalk down Main Street.

Want to meet me at Ben's for a quick breakfast? I texted.

It didn't take him too long to text back, telling me he'd already gotten to Clay's Ferry, and he'd see me tonight at the town council meeting.

The thought of the meeting made my stomach curl. The fact I was going to have to defend myself wasn't something I had planned on worrying with.

The Tattered Cover Book and Inn was the only place to stay in downtown Cottonwood. The inn outside of town was the other. Both filled up pretty quickly, and from what I'd heard from the rumblings at the wedding, both places were completely booked.

"You stay right here," I told Duke and gave him a good scratch on his head. He sat down in front of the hotel before he dropped down to lie on the concrete already warmed up from the sun.

Nanette, the owner and operator of the hotel, who took great pride in offering refreshments and cold iced tea to her inn guests, was in what I called the refreshment room. It was a room located to the right as soon as you walked through the front door of the inn.

She was busying herself at the bar where she had small breakfast offerings for her guests. Food like hard-boiled eggs, fruit, bagels, toast, and all sorts of juices and coffee.

"Good morning, Kenni." She turned around with a large smile on her face. "I thought I was going to be spending the rest of this week cleaning up from the wedding guests. I understand a few of them are staying because you aren't letting them leave."

"I'm sure you've heard all sorts of things, Nanette." I smiled. "How are you doing?"

"Fine. My sciatica has been hurting, going up and down the steps. It's been hard to find any good help these days." She put her hand on the small of her back and pressed on it. "Are you here to question some of the guests? I can clean up real fast and let you use this room."

"That's a generous offer, but I'm here to see Bradley Ines." I pointed to the steps that led up to the rooms. "Do you recall his room number off the top of your head?"

"Five." She held up her hand. "I know because he had the bachelor party after-party here, and I had many complaints that night." She snorted. "That morning."

The front desk phone rang.

"I've got to get that." She hurried out of the room without me able to ask her what she was talking about.

Instead of waiting on her and asking her about that night, I decided to make a stop to see her before I left to get the details in case they were important. I went ahead and walked up the steps to where the rooms were located. I made my way down to room five and gave the already cracked-open door a little knock.

"Bradley," I called into the crack. "It's Sheriff Lowry. Can we have a quick talk?"

I took a step back and stared at the door with my hands resting on my utility belt.

Nothing.

I reached out again and knocked a couple of swift times with my knuckle. I pulled my hand in and rested it on the utility belt again.

Nothing.

I looked down the hall both ways before I decided to take a step forward and give one last knock, this time hard enough to open the door enough to see inside.

This time there was something.

"He's heard his last crow." Poppa appeared over my shoulder.

Bradley Ines was lying on the floor, blood pouring out of his head.

CHAPTER EIGHTEEN

"Anything?" I asked Max Bogus when he walked out of the room after he declared Bradley Ines was in fact. . . dead.

"Blow to the head. Didn't see it coming." He shook his head. "I'll send over a final once I get a better look at the body."

"Thanks." I nodded and looked over at Nanette. She was crying uncontrollably at the top of the stairs.

After I'd found Bradley, I'd called in backup, which was Scott, before I made a phone call downstairs to the Tattered Cover Book and Inn desk from my phone. When I'd asked Nanette to come up, she immediately bolted up the steps. I told her what had happened in room number five, and she'd not stopped crying since.

It wasn't until after she'd watched Max Bogus and one of his employees carry Bradley's body out that she started hyperventilating.

Since I didn't have my Jeep parked right outside of the hotel, I had to tell Scott to bring a camera and his deputy bag so we could collect evidence and process the scene.

"I just can't believe this." She used a piece of torn-up tissue paper to wipe her seeping nose and wet eyes. "He seemed like such a nice boy too. He was the life of the party. Even last night when they were—" She clamped her lips to stop whatever it was she was about to say.

"They were? Who were? What were?" I asked.

"It was all in good fun. Really, Kenni." Nanette was preparing me for something. I gave her a tight smile. "I mean, he had you down pat."

"He was mocking me?" I didn't mind good fun. I could take it. "He was pretending to be me? To whom?" I asked to her nod.

"The wedding party. They were all in the refreshment room having some pizza, and I thought they were play charades." Her hand fluttered. "You know that game where—"

"I know the game." I interrupted her.

"You should've heard—" She stopped talking. Her brows pinched. "I mean he sounded just like—" She stopped again. "What happened to him?"

"The wedding party is here?" I didn't realize they were staying in this one particular place since they'd already come down to the station to give their statements. I figured they were all gone by now.

"Yes. They are leaving tomorrow. They told me last night they couldn't get a flight out today and they were hoping Bradley was cleared." Nanette knew more than she'd initially let on when I first walked into the inn.

"You know. I overhear things." She gave a quick shake to her head.

"I'm going to need to keep room five locked tight until we can get all the evidence collected we need. You do understand, don't you?" I noticed Scott pop his head out of the door.

"Yes." Nanette's face grew solemn. "Can I do anything?"

"I'd appreciate it if you didn't give any statements to anyone or tell anyone about this." Nanette was also a part of the gossip circle in Cottonwood. "We don't want the killer to know our next move. Or what we know."

She nodded with a determined look on her face before she headed back down the steps.

I took a deep breath in order to clear my head from one conversation to the one I was about to have with Deputy Lee.

"Did you find anything?" I asked Scott after I walked into the room.

"Cash. Lots of it." He pulled open the small wooden desk drawer. The desk was sitting in front of a window facing Main Street.

"I think we need to print," I told Scott. He pointed to his bag on the bed. I walked over and pulled out a pair of gloves and the dusting powder inside.

Dusting for prints was a tedious and messy job.

"The money. Check the sequence of bills." Poppa made a good point. "Then we need to go back to the bank to see if those came from there."

"Or I need to talk to the wedding party again." I nibbled on my lip as more theories popped into my head.

"What?" Scott asked.

"I was just thinking out loud." My brows pinched. "When you talked to Jasmine and Dickie, did they say anything to you about Bradley?"

"No. They've been friends since college. You knew that. Are you thinking it was one of them?" Scott asked.

"I'm thinking it's got to be someone in the wedding party, unless Brenda had come here last night." My mind twirled with reasons Brenda had a motive to not only kill her husband, but now Bradley. "Have you gotten any word on the warrant for the bank?"

"Not that I've seen." He looked at his watch. "It could be there now."

I gave Scott the powder to continue to dust for prints while I made a walkie-talkie call to the department.

I reached up to the walkie-talkie strapped onto my shoulder and clicked the button. "Hey, Betty." I looked out the front window of the room and down to the sidewalk. Duke was still sitting there like a good boy.

"Sheriff." Her voice screeched over the intercom.

"Did you see a warrant come over the fax for the Cottonwood First National Bank?" I clicked off.

"I heard the fax go off, but I'd not checked it yet. Hold on." She clicked off. I waited in the hall while she got up to look, knowing it would take her a minute to get her footing, grab her glasses, and go check the fax.

There'd been a small gathering down the hall. All of the guests were facing toward room five. I didn't recognize any of them as the wedding party. But I still wanted to talk to the bride and groom.

The walkie-talkie beeped to life. "Yes. It's right here."

"Thanks, Betty. I'll be right over to get it and drop Duke off." I clicked off the walkie-talkie and headed down the steps. "Nanette." I tapped the counter to grab her attention. "Can you tell me what room the Dees are in?"

"The honeymoon suite on the third floor." She caught me off guard. "What? They are on their honeymoon, even though their best friend is. . ." Her voice fluttered off, as did her gaze.

"I didn't realize you had a honeymoon suite." I pointed. "Top of the stairs then what?"

"Oh no." She plucked a tissue from the box sitting on the counter. She dabbed her eyes. "You have to go around the back to the alley. There's an old elevator car to take you up there. Very romantic."

"Okay." I walked out the door. Duke jumped to his feet, and we walked down the street, taking the road leading to the alley of the department so I could grab the warrant.

"Kenni." Polly Parker Ryland ran out of White's Jewelry. "Kenni, I was wanting to speak with you for a minute." She rubbed her belly.

"I'm sorry, Polly, can I come back later?" I asked but thought "later" as in "much later, like a year."

Polly worked for Viola at the jewelry store, which was right up Polly's alley. She loved and wore anything that sparkled and had her initials engraved on it. Much like Viola, Polly's fingers were lined with the best of stones.

"It'll take just a second." She swung the jewelry store door open.

The gray awning above the double doors of the shop flapped in the light breeze. White's Jewelry was written in calligraphy across the front windows of the shop with two solitaire diamond outlines on each side.

"Really, Polly, I am." I was walking and talking at the same time to hurry past her.

"I'll tell Chance to lay off harassing you about the—" She slid her head right and then left before she put her hand up to the side of her mouth and whispered, "Murders."

"Murderssss?" I made the plural very obvious.

"Mmhmmm." Her perfectly lined pinky lips hummed. "Nanette told me about the best man. You scratch my back, I scratch yours. Or at least keep Chance off of your back."

She pushed the door open a little wider, holding the bottom with her foot.

"Fine." How long could whatever she had to say take? "Stay," I told Duke.

He let out a low grumble before he dropped to his belly, letting the late-morning sun give him a little sunbath.

"What's going on?" I stood right inside of the jewelry store. The glass counters around the perimeter of the inside glistened with all sorts of sparkly baubles.

"Do you like any of these?" She gushed over one of the counters that had a sign on top of it that read Here Comes the Bride. "What about a pear shape?" She swung her hands overtop of the display as if she were on that show, *The Price Is Right*.

"Polly, I'm sorry. What is it that you wanted?" I asked. "Not that I don't like visiting with you, but I'm a little busy."

"I know, the murders and all, but I was just thinking." She had a nervous look on her face I'd not recognized. It was as if she were trying to come up with something on the spot.

"Spit it out." God knew she has those fancy veneers in her mouth to spit anything out, I thought to myself.

"Will you have a baby shower for me?" she blurted.

"I, um. . ." I stuttered for the words, trying to figure out why of all people in her life she'd ask me.

I started sweatin' like a pig who knew he was for supper.

She shifted her weight back and forth on her feet.

"Of course." I had to get out of there. She was making me nervous now. "Yes. I'd love to. I'll have it at the church. The auxiliary women will be delighted to help."

"Thank you." The Southern dripped out of her mouth like thick honey. "You're the best, Kenni! I'll repay you when you have a bridal shower," she called out to me on my way out the door.

"Oh!" I turned around. "I'm not into fancy diamonds." I shrugged. "I think I want my grandmother's ring to wear when I get married."

I pushed out the door into the sunlight. Duke jumped to his feet. I glanced back right before the jewelry store door slowly closed. Polly's petite nose was curled, as was the edge of her top lip.

"Last stop." I scratched and led the charge down the street. "Who cares about a ring?" I said to Duke.

"I'll tell you this, that boy ain't getting your granny's ring," Poppa protested. "I'll never tell them where it is."

"Come to think about it," I talked to Duke so no one would think I'd lost my marbles.

Heck, maybe I had. Maybe Poppa wasn't there and the loss of him even after all of these years still had an effect on me.

Maybe.

I shrugged and went on anyways.

"I have never thought about the ring since I moved into your house." My mind circled back to some years ago, and how I'd found it in Poppa's bedside table. A table I'd opened many times since then.

Daily, to be exact.

I kept my gun in there, when in reality I should've immediately put it in the gun safe, but you never knew about Free Row. At any given moment, a gunshot in the air was exactly what the rebels living on Free Row needed when they got a little rowdy at night and hopped up on too much juice.

If you knew what I meant.

"Don't you worry about it. When the time is right, I'll present the ring in a place where the right man can find it." Poppa was making my decision to get married or not to Finn easier than I could've hoped.

"I'm sure it'll all work out fine." I turned the corner of the building and headed down the alley. "Marriage is not on Finn's radar, anyways."

There was no way I was going to bring up this morning, when Finn had stopped by and heard me yelling at Mama and Viola about me and marriage.

Something I didn't want to think about, nor had time or the head space.

"Any news from Max?" I asked Betty as soon as I walked in the department door.

"Hello to you too, Duke." Betty took the lid off the treat jar. She took one out and gave it to Duke. She rubbed his back while he ate it. "Good boy for using good manners."

"Okay. Hello, Betty." I got the hint loud and clear.

"Oh, hi, Sheriff." Betty's beady eyes snapped at me. "Just because you're the big cheese around here, still doesn't mean you can't use manners. And no. Nothing from Max, but your mama called. She heard about Bradley and insists you call her."

"She did." I looked at the fax from the judge on my desk to make sure it was the exact warrant I needed for the bank.

"Mmhmmm." Betty hummed.

"I mean she heard about Bradley?" Betty didn't look up at me. "Or someone here told her about Bradley?"

"Kenni, you know that I'm part of the prayer chain for the church, and when I heard the call come through, I had to start praying for him. Regardless if he killed Gary or not, he still needs praying for." Betty typed away on the computer.

It appeared she was typing in the report from the witness statements.

"Did you come across the statement from Jasmine and Dickie Dee yet?" I asked and folded the warrant then put it in my jacket pocket.

"I just finished typing it." She peered at me from overtop her reading glasses.

"And nothing stuck out to you?" I would pore over them later this afternoon when I got back from the bank and my little visit with Brenda Futch.

"There was one event that stood out from the groomsmen."

"Yeah? What was that?" I asked.

"They said the bachelor party got a little out of hand, and they all smiled fondly." Betty had my attention. "When Scott asked Dickie about it, he put a note on the report that Dickie didn't want to discuss it now that he was married."

"Did anyone say when the bachelor party was?" I wondered. "Preacher Bing mentioned something about a bachelor party when I questioned him about the premarital counseling sessions."

I flipped through Gary's file and looked at the photos we'd taken of the cash from his pocket.

"No, but I can find out." Betty grabbed the phone and waved me off. She moved the receiver down past her chin and said, "I'll let you know."

"Duke is staying here." I gestured and mouthed the words because she started talking to the person on the other end of the phone.

She nodded two quick times and waved me out with her free hand.

Since my Jeep was already down at the Cottonwood First National Bank and I needed some thinking time, I took my time walking down the alley which would bring me to West Oak. I went ahead and jogged my way across the street, where I took a right to walk down the sidewalk and left into the bank parking lot.

It was like Vernon Bishop was waiting on me when I walked in.

He waved me on into his office.

"I got a call from the judge. I figured you'd be here soon." Vernon pulled some papers off the printer behind him. "Here is Brenda's account. Here is a sum of money she deposited as soon as the bank opened. I'm guessing you wanted those serial numbers too."

"How did you know?" I asked and looked to where he was pointing his finger.

Oddly familiar. I pulled my phone out of my pocket and thumbed through to my email where Max had mentioned he'd emailed photos of the cash in Gary's pocket. Though I knew the cash Brenda had deposited wasn't the same since Gary's cash was in an evidence bag in lockup, it would be interesting if there were some similar numbers.

"My goodness." I couldn't contain the shock. "These are in the same serial number family. Which tells me whoever gave Gary the money in his pocket came from the same place."

"How do you know it wasn't Brenda?" Vernon asked. "I guess she got it from someone since we don't have that serial sequence here before her deposit. Maybe she gave Gary some?"

"Could've." My eyes scanned down Brenda's bank statements. "She makes large deposits every other day."

Vernon's chair creaked when he sat back. His fingers folded, and his elbows tented out and rested on the arms of his chair.

"I don't see a business on here." I thumbed through the papers.

"That's her only account. It's a personal one."

"You mentioned her business. I'm assuming a woman would run one like Mary Kay or Tupperware." I was fishing for some answers.

"Yes. She's a businesswoman." Vernon shrugged. "She does that whole quarterly tax thing, I guess."

"Have you ever seen her come in here with anyone else?" I asked.

"Maybe one or two of the girls that work under her." He didn't seem like he was too concerned or worried about it.

"Thanks, Vernon." I had no idea why I was thanking him since I had to get a warrant, but like I had with Betty earlier, I guessed it was best to play nice. Especially since I knew Vernon would be at the council meeting tonight.

"Kenni, um, Sheriff Lowry," Betty's voice cracked over the walkie-talkie.

"Excuse me." I took the papers, folded them up, and stuck them in my back pocket as I headed out the door to talk back to answer Betty's dispatch. "I'm here."

"So is Janice Gallo. She's ranting and raving about her client, Bradley Ines, and demanding to talk to you." Betty's voice twitched with nervousness.

"You can tell her I'm out of the office doing my job, and we can talk at the town council meeting." I clicked off and scrolled the volume button down.

There was no way I was going to let Janice Gallo run my investigation now that her client was dead. I was the sheriff, and this was my town.

She was going to have to deal with me tonight at the town council meeting.

CHAPTER NINETEEN

With Brenda Futch in mind, I got back into my Wagoneer and pulled out left on Main Street from West Oak, headed back to Liberty Street where the Futches lived.

I wasn't sure what I was going to say to her, other than what was her job and where did she get all this money.

There were some answers that needed to be heard, and I knew she was a missing link, if not the link.

I pushed the walkie-talkie button and scrolled up the volume. "Deputy Lee."

"Go ahead, Sheriff."

"I am heading over to Liberty Street to talk to Brenda Futch. Are you in the vicinity?" Not that he would be far. We could reach each side of town in ten minutes going at a snail's pace.

"I can be. On my way." He clicked off.

The On The Run food truck was pulled up tight to the curb in front of Lulu's Boutique. Which made me think of Lulu McClain, which made me think of Mama and Viola getting tracker information from Tiny Tina's.

I glanced at the arms on the old clock on the Wagoneer dashboard and knew Tiny Tina's was open, but the gossip didn't get started until well into the afternoon. That was when everyone was fully caffeinated, with their lips flapping a million miles a minute.

It was something I had to mentally prepare myself for. It was the weeding through all the gossip to find bits and pieces of the truth that exhausted me.

But first I had to deal with Brenda. More importantly, how she was connected to Bradley.

"What are you doing here?" Brenda's voice carried past me, as did her gaze. "I have already given my statement to Deputy Scott Lee, just like you said. Now what do you want?"

"We can either talk about this out here." I looked behind me. There was a group of neighbors who'd gathered on the lawn across the street. They didn't even try to cover up their stares. "Or we can go inside where there's a little more privacy, so we can discuss your banking business and the large deposits you've been making at the Cottonwood First National Bank."

I grabbed the warrant from my back pocket and with a good flick of my wrist unfolded the paper.

She leaned in and took a look.

"It's a warrant I used to get your bank records." I pulled the bank records I'd gotten from Vernon out of my other back pocket and handed them to her, leaving it to her to open them.

"I have reason to believe you and your husband knew my new victim. And what you and your husband had to do with the Dees' wedding." I stood there waiting for the invite to go inside.

I had no reason not to conduct my business on her front porch, so I continued, because apparently she didn't care who heard our business. The hedges between her house and the next-door neighbor's shook to life. I glanced over and realized we now had an audience listening in from all sides.

"It's been brought to my attention your husband was stabbed with Bradley's umbrella. Plus eyewitnesses had identified Bradley Ines walking in and out of your house before he was killed." She still didn't budge. Brenda looked at me with a blank face. I got louder. "I have reason to believe you and Bradley are in some sort of tangled-up web, and well, I'm going to find out exactly what that is."

There was a glimmer of anger in her eyes, giving me a little hope she was going to take this inside.

"I can keep going, and much louder, for everyone here on Liberty Street to hear me if you'd like." I gave Brenda a second to think about it before I opened my mouth.

"Fine." She closed her eyes in frustration before she sucked in a deep breath, letting it out as she used the toe of her shoe to hold the storm door open. "You can come in."

I took the first step inside and walked into a family room with a couple of couches, chairs, and a television that was on the local station. There were two women sitting on the couch, and they quickly got up to go into the other room.

"Family? Friends?" I asked.

"Employees," she said with a flat tone.

"Oh."

I heard the ghost of my poppa before I saw him sprinkle himself in ghost form on the other side of the room. "I know where I recognize Gary from."

I'd forgotten all about how Poppa had made mention of recognizing him when he saw Gary lying there at the reception.

"It's the oldest business around." Poppa shook his head. "I arrested them a few times down on the town branch."

"Oldest business?" I asked out loud. "That's what Vernon said."

Brenda slowly looked over her shoulder to where Poppa was standing and turned back to me with big eyes.

"Who are you talking to?" She shivered.

"I never arrested them, just tried to get them off the street. Didn't look good for Cottonwood, and Gary insisted it was an up-and-up business. Sex will never be banished." Poppa had a way.

"Here I thought you sold cosmetics." I scoffed at my naivety. "What exactly is your business, before I jump to any conclusions?"

"I own a sorta dating service." Brenda sat down on the edge of the couch and gestured me to sit.

"Is that what we are calling it these days?" I asked.

"I run a legitimate escort business. All my employees are offered health insurance and other benefits." She tugged on a footstool next to the couch and opened a secret file cabinet. "You can look through any of the files. No warrant necessary."

"Why didn't you disclose any of this information to Deputy Lee?" I wondered, sitting back on the couch and pulling out my notebook and my phone from the front pocket of my shirt.

"He didn't ask what my occupation or business is." She was a sneaky one.

"Sheriff Kendrick Lowry interviewing Brenda Futch." I had hit the record button on the memo app of my phone and set it on the arm of the couch closest to Brenda. "Why don't you start from the beginning to when you were first contacted by Bradley Ines."

It had become increasingly clear this had to do with Bradley and the escort service. This was the tie between the two victims I'd been trying to get at for the last forty-eight hours, almost.

"Would you like something to drink?" she asked, as if we were here for story hour.

I declined. "Just start at the beginning," I encouraged her. Since I'd learned of what she was loosely calling an escort service, my suspect pool just got a little bigger.

I had no idea what was going to come out of Brenda's mouth. What if one of her girls killed Gary and then Bradley? This was going to shake down and shake down now.

Poppa had ghosted himself next to me. He was ready to listen.

"Time sure hasn't been kind to her." Poppa eyeballed Brenda. "They were young when they started out this business, and many times I had to arrest them. Put him in the clink for a night or two."

I shifted, so Poppa would get the hint to hush so I could listen.

"My business is no different than any dating app three-fourths of Cottonwood has downloaded on their phone." Brenda had taken the defensive side right off. "About two months ago, one of my employees got into a little trouble. We needed a lawyer, so Gary and I spent a lot of what we had in fees to help her out. Gary had taken a part-time job at That's a Toast catering service with Venetta Stenner to help pay some of the bills."

Brenda looked at me from up underneath her brows.

"A couple of months ago." I restarted her tale for her.

"Yes. We were sitting right here. That's when I got a call from Bradley Ines. He said he was the best man in a wedding taking place locally, and they were coming to town for a bachelor party. He also said he'd dropped the ball, and this was a last-minute booking for a little fun. Now, for the right price, we were able to offer him a package that suited his needs. Since Gary and I were in a bit of a pinch, as was Bradley with his timing, we didn't find it unnecessary to charge him a little more, seeing how we had to pull some of our best employees for the job."

I was so glad she'd left out what skills her best employees had.

"Bradley's group was the handsy type. If you know what I mean." She crossed one leg over the other, dangling her foot in the air. "Nothing illegal. Just immoral, if you catch my drift, and it was my employees' fault too. So I can't blame Bradley and that crew."

She paused and looked out into the room.

"One of my girls fell head over heels in love with the groom, Dickie. So much so they'd even started a little fling over the past couple of months. He thought it was a fling, but my employee did not. Unfortunately with cell phones these days, one of my employees took photos of the bachelor party and started to blackmail Dickie after he'd tried to call if off with my girl."

I could see this playing out since I knew a couple of the characters involved.

"I don't see it as blackmail as much as him paying her for her escort services, so when Bradley Ines called Gary about the blackmail, Gary told him such."

"He told him to think of the blackmail as paying for her services?" I wanted to be very clear because this was something I was going to have to go talk to Dickie Dee about, and that was a whole nother can of worms to open.

"We don't think of it as blackmail. He used her for services, and we saw it as services rendered. We also told Bradley and Dickie they needed to hire That's a Toast for the reception, so we could get the last payment in exchange for the photos."

"That's why Gary worked for Venetta." I shook my head. "And that's why he had all the cash on him. I'd like to see the photos."

"Gary handed them off to Bradley when they were at the wedding reception," she said. "Our business with those two were done."

"I don't recall seeing any photos at Bradley's hotel." Scott and I had combed the place. There weren't any photos.

"Then Dickie has them. That's not my problem. Bradley came over here to let me know our business was done and that he didn't kill my husband." She was talking about the time Mama and Viola had tracked him here.

"What about your employees who had to do with all this?" I asked. "Are they available to talk to Deputy Lee, and do they have an alibi for the nights in question for both of my victims?"

"Yes. I have all their on-duty records as well as cell phone pings. I told you, I keep a close eye on my escort business. I am more than happy to have them talk to him." She was so confident in her delivery of her story, I truly found myself believing every word as she told it.

"What about you? It seems like the killer is plucking off victims one at a time in fear they might tell the secret of Dickie's affair. Aren't you worried you're next?" I asked.

"I never thought of it." Her brows pinched, as though the realization she could be the next victim was a real possibility.

"Didn't Preacher Bing mention something about Dickie taking over Jasmine's father's business and an argument there?" Poppa reminded me of what I'd considered a silly argument, but it turned out it wasn't so silly, after all.

"Yes, but not if those photos get out or a whisper of what he's done to Jasmine gets out." I knew firsthand what type of poppa bear Jasmine's dad was. It was him leading the charge to sue me and the city of Cottonwood because I ruined the wedding reception.

"Looks like we got one on the line, Kenni bug." Poppa rubbed his hands vigorously together.

"What?" Brenda uncurled her legs and inched up to the edge of the couch.

"I'm talking to myself." My eyes narrowed. I stood up. "I have to go, but I'll call Deputy Lee to come here and take the statements of your employees. We will need to do a check on them, but I also want him to sit out front. Make sure no one comes to pay you any unwanted visits while I'm buttoning up who killed your husband."

"I don't think it would do too good for business if you planted a Cottonwood deputy's car out front of my business." What she was saying was loud and clear.

"What if it was a few houses down?" I offered.

"That would be fine." She blinked a few times, and a sadness fell upon her face. "I do hope you find out who killed Gary and Bradley."

"I think I'm on the right track." I let myself out of the house and got in the Jeep.

Instead of calling Scott on the walkie-talkie and letting the dispatch, Betty, hear what I'd found out, since I needed to make sure it was kept under wraps and not let out to the entire prayer chain, I called him.

After I dialed Scott's number, I put the phone up to my ear and stared out the windshield down Liberty Street. With my free hand, I cranked the manual window down to let in some fresh air. It was a gorgeous spring day, and fresh air was always good for the brain. Right now my brain was reeling with ideas on how I was going to get in front of Dickie without Jasmine and her father hammering down on me.

"Hey, Scott. I wanted to call you instead of going over dispatch." I was about to tell him everything I'd found out about Brenda and Gary's business when I looked at the car driving slowly past.

As if in slow motion, the driver of the other vehicle turned their head as they were passing me. The eyes blinked open, and we stared at each other, lingering for a moment too long as we realized who each other was.

Then time sped up and fast. The engine of his car roared to life when he punched the gas and zoomed down the street.

"Dickie Dee," I gasped. "He's driving past the Futches'. I need you to get to the Futches'." I jammed the phone between my ear and shoulder, pulling the gear shift into Drive and making a U-turn in the middle of the road, barely missing the car parked across the street.

"Dickie Dee was being blackmailed by Gary Futch." I gave Scott just enough information to make it dire for him to drop everything and get over there now. "My fear is Dickie is trying to silence anyone who knows what is going on. And I can't help but to think if Jasmine's father knew, Dickie would be out of the family business for good."

Scott and I hung up the phone as soon as I rounded the corner of Liberty where it met Cemetery Road. I threw the phone on the passenger seat. With one hand on the wheel and eyes on Dickie's taillights, I reached under my seat and pulled out the old beacon police siren.

I brought the siren's suction cup up to my mouth and licked it before I put it out the window and stuck it up on the roof of my Jeep. My finger slid down the side of the light and flipped the switch on, bringing the loud siren to life and making the light flash.

With both hands on the wheel, I maneuvered the old Wagoneer through the winding, single-lane road in the cemetery, hot on Dickie's bumper.

His car was a little four-door, which made it easier for him to get around the cars parked along the edge of the tombstones where their owners were visiting with their loved ones.

"Whoa!" Even Poppa's ghost was hanging on tight to the arm of the door. "Don't be hitting no one or no stones."

"I'm not." I had to slow down a smidgen when we got to an active graveside service.

"This is a send-off." Poppa's sick sense of humor about me barreling through, practically ruining the service for whoever was being laid to rest, wasn't sitting well with me.

"I don't like this at all." I kept the wheel steady even though my heart rapidly beat to the small breaths I was taking in. "We are coming to the front and then on Main Street."

It was like I had a premonition of what was going to happen.

"If someone doesn't let him out of the cemetery, I'm afraid he'll just pull out in front of them." I didn't have to finish my thought about him hitting someone's car in the process because just as I said it, Dickie jerked a right out of the cemetery, barely missing getting hit by a car going northbound on Main Street.

By the time I got to the entrance of the cemetery and the oncoming traffic heard the siren and had stopped, Dickie had already zoomed past Ruby's Antiques and turned left off Main onto Richmond Avenue, where I knew he'd be heading for the country. Not a risk I was going to take to lose him there. He could easily slip onto a small gravel country road, hide in the brush, and wait me out all day.

"Dang." I beat the stirring wheel with the palm of my hand and pulled over at the rear of Cottonwood Cleaners.

"You'll get him. He can't hide forever, especially with the lawyer coming tonight to the town council meeting. I know Jasmine's dad is going to be there about the lawsuit. Then you can spring it on them." Poppa had always been able to play it really cool when it came to hauling in suspects, but in the case of Dickie, he ran from me, and that itself was criminal enough for me to bring his heinie in and make him sit in jail.

"Tonight." One by one I peeled my fingers off the stirring wheel, keeping my palms on it. I looked at each one of my fingernails. I moved my gaze to the rearview mirror and took in the woolly worms sitting above my eyes, better known as my thick eyebrows. "I could stand a good manicure and brow wax."

"And some good homespun gossip." Poppa reminded me just how much I could learn from my little break at the local salon, where I was guaranteed to hear something I'd not yet heard. "And Ruby did give you her time slot if you needed it."

"Then Tiny Tina's it is." I put the Jeep in Drive and took a left out of the Cottonwood Cleaners parking lot to get back on Main Street.

Tiny Tina's was located in the strip mall along with the dentist's office, The Pawn, Cottonwood Federal Savings, Hart's insurance office, and a Subway. A few of the rockers that lined the front of the strip mall shops were already occupied by customers' spouses. When I pulled up, it was hard not to notice all of their eyes on me, wondering what on earth the sheriff was doing there.

I'd called Scott back on my way there to let him know exactly what had happened and why I was headed to the salon.

"I want to talk to the bride," I told Poppa. "I'm not sure why they aren't on their honeymoon, and I'm not sure why Dickie ran from me, other than guilt."

"We need to think about it. What if he told Bradley Ines to take care of everything? Bradley was still in love with Jasmine. Maybe Bradley was doing his own sort of blackmailing with all the information."

"What a tangled web they weave." I sighed and turned the engine off. "Let's go see what we can find out in here."

I grabbed the door handle and swept the door open. The hum of hairdryers, hissing of aerosol sprays, and smell of astringent cleaners and chemical hair dyes, mixed in with chatter, told me Tiny Tina's was full of life.

"Hey, Kenni!" Tina Bowers, the owner of Tiny Tina's, was all the way in the back of the salon, sitting on a low-to-the-ground stool in front of Polly Parker Ryland.

Tina's hands were rubbing Polly's shins, slathering on her specialty rub. Really it was lotion she'd gotten down at Dixon's Foodtown. She fancied it with drops of vanilla extract before she put it in small bottles she'd bought off the internet and slapped on some labels she'd printed off herself, making it her own brand of spa lotion.

I waved my hand in front of my face after a big spray of something made its way into my mouth.

"Pftt, pftt." I spit and rubbed my nose.

"Ruby told me you might be in," Tina called out with a big smile.

Tina loved getting her fingers all tangled up in my hair, which happened about twice a year at most. Honestly, my hair was pretty much always worn up in a ponytail, and fixing it wasn't high on my list. This was why Mama used it as a good example for losing Finn.

She claimed in order to keep a good man like Finn, I had to keep up my appearance. That wasn't how I felt, and it certainly wasn't how Finn had made me feel, but for the sake of the murders, I was willing to let Tina Bowers shampoo, blow-dry, and snip—whatever needed to be done to find the killer.

"Ladies," I greeted everyone when I walked around the counter and past the group of ladies under the pink hair dryers with their curlers snugged tight to their heads.

The sound of scissors snipping and a dry broom sweeping across the floor mixed in with laughs and stories.

"Sheriff." Each one of them stopped telling their tales and nodded with pinched smiles as I passed.

"Polly. Just the woman I wanted to see. I'm glad you're here." I sat down in the pedicure chair next to her, allowing my body to sink into the pleather chair.

"You have? What on earth do you want with me?" Polly lifted her petite hand to her chest.

"I'm going to need your help with getting your husband off my back." I knew if anyone could talk to the mayor, it was his own wife.

I planted my forearm on the arm of the spa chair and leaned over a little closer to Polly.

"I'm going to need a little more time to get the case solved, and with Chance breathing down my neck, I'm afraid he's making it a little more difficult for all the people who I need to have cooperate." I had no idea what Chance had been telling people, but I knew he could make tonight's town council meeting go smoother if he wanted to.

"Now, Kenni, you and I both know Chance is his own man." Polly shook her head. Her freshly cut short blond bob waved back and forth, not a hair out of place. No doubt Tina had plastered the strands with high-hold hair spray.

"We both know you wear the pants and Chance would do anything for you." I'd been a witness to this courtship and marriage. She knew what I was saying was true.

My brows rose when I took a look at the phone in her hand.

She slid it to the side of her leg, slipping it underneath as if I didn't see her.

"I had asked for your photos from your phone from the wedding, but when I got back to the office and looked through Deputy Lee's list of wedding guests who sent in their photos, you weren't checked off." I sighed. "That's not cooperating with the sheriff, and as the first lady of Cottonwood, you do want to make sure everyone knows that you are cooperating with me to keep Cottonwood safe."

She pushed her back into the pleather just enough for it to let out a little squeak.

"I don't mind you looking at my photos right now." She jerked the phone up from underneath her leg and used her shiny, newly painted red fingernail to tap it to life.

Tina glanced up from in between Polly's feet and smiled with a wink. She had her hair pulled up in a topknot, and it shook back and forth as she ground the pumice stone on the heels of Polly's feet. The dry skin sprinkled all over the black towel in Tina's lap like falling snow.

She batted the pad of her finger on the screen until she was satisfied she had found what she was looking for and then shoved the phone into my face.

"Here you go." Polly handed me the phone. "Swipe right."

Tina put Polly's feet back into the foot spa. The water bubbled to life after Tina flipped on the switch.

"Oh Tina." Polly laid the back of her head on the pillow attached to the back of the chair. "This is heaven."

I could hear Polly's feet moving around the rocks Tina had put into the foot spa tubs like Tiny Tina's was some fancy, high-dollar salon with their little marbles and crystals. The only person who knew those rocks were dug out from the town branch was me, her, and the woman who'd called dispatch to tell me Tina was trespassing and stealing rocks from the creek.

I told Tina we wouldn't press charges if she stopped stealing rocks and telling everyone the rocks she used at the spa were fancy. I'd not heard a word since.

"How many photos did you take?" I asked, my eyes glazing over when all the photos started to look the same.

One after the other of Jasmine, a few of the entire bridal party, but none of the waiter or Bradley Ines that I could see. Even when I used my fingers to pinch the photo bigger, there was nothing.

"You can never take too many because if you don't, then you might miss something." Polly used her finger to suggest me to flip forward. "If you look at those centerpieces, those will be perfect for the Winter Jam."

"Winter Jam?" Tina got a little excited. Her voice went up an octave. "What is that?" Tina patted Polly's leg and stood up, gesturing for me to follow her.

"Something extra special for Cottonwood that I'm personally overseeing." Polly loved being part of every single club in Cottonwood. That was really her full-time job. Her little part-time gig at White's Jewelry was just a hobby for her.

"I'm going to text myself a few of these." I quickly tapped on Select and hit a few of the reception where I'd noticed Mama's table and the umbrella sitting on it. It looked as though Mama didn't leave the umbrella outside like I thought she would've.

If the umbrella was still inside, how did it get into Gary's dead body? That would mean Max Bogus's assessment of the umbrella being left outside was not right.

"Come on, Kenni, I've got a full day." Tina's patience was being tested. "We've got to get some of those golden highlights touched up, and those brows." She tsk-tsked. "It's a shame too. You've got such pretty green eyes. You cover them up with those brows."

"I like her brows." Polly looked up, batting her long fake lashes. "Thick brows are coming back in style."

"See there, Tina," I teased and sent myself a few more photos before I got up. "If I wait long enough, I'll be in total style."

"Heaven help us." Tina's words weren't ones of flattery.

CHAPTER TWENTY

I barely had enough time to make it to the town council meeting before it started. By the time Tina let loose of my hair, it'd been a few hours. My scalp hurt from all the chemicals, hair brushing, curling iron, and products she'd used on it. I was sure my hair was in its own kinda shock.

The skin between my eyes and underneath my eyebrows was bright red. It was as if each eyebrow had its own heartbeat, because they thumped in pain.

Just a little more here and here was what Tina had said as she applied the hot wax and ripped it right off. I knew I should've been worried when she didn't have any sort of instrument to apply the melted liquid and made me eat a Popsicle that looked like it'd been in the freezer for years so she could use the stick to apply the wax.

My stomach ached, and I was sure it was from the old Popsicle that Tina proclaimed had what was called protective covering. It was freezer rot to me.

Still, I let her do it for the sake of the investigation and to keep Polly entertained so she'd get Chance to lay off my back.

When I finally walked into Luke and Vita Joneses' basement, I barely made it just as Chance Ryland was bringing the meeting to order.

"This session is in order!" Mayor Ryland stood behind the podium in the front of Luke's basement. He banged the wooden gavel. "Let's get this meeting started."

He glanced over at Toots Buford, who had found her a new part-time job taking the minutes of the weekly meetings. I tried to attend most of them, but some days it was just easier than others. Today it seemed as if the entire town had come out to see what the word was on the murders.

Chance slid his eyes up to the back where I was standing.

"We'd like to call Sheriff Lowry to the podium so she can give us an update on the double homicide. I'm sure she'll give us some peace." I followed his eyes as they moved to the front row where Polly was smiling, her big veneers boldly glowing as she smiled at her husband.

Obviously she'd talked to him after she left the salon.

All the folding metal chairs were filled, and as I wove my way around them, I noticed practically everyone I knew was there.

Camille, Ben, Viola, and Ruby were seated in the second row. The Kims, along with their daughter and my friend Gina, were sitting in the first row with Mama and Daddy, who were seated next to Polly.

Mama gave me a little silent clap. My dad sat proud next to her, smiling.

"Go get 'em, Kenni bug." Poppa gave me a double thumbs-up and a toothy grin.

I stepped up in front of everyone and noticed Jasmine Dee, her daddy, and Janice sitting in the third row.

Edna Easterly wasn't hard to spot. She knelt down in the front. The feathered fedora choice for tonight's meeting was a lime-green number. The feather was a foot taller than any head in the crowd. The darn thing waved in the air as her head bobbled back and forth as she tried to get her handheld tape recorder as close to me as possible.

Luke Jones was busy trying to get the pull-down movie screen in the rolled-up position as he jerked on the bottom of it a couple of times. It was being moody.

"It's fine," Chance told Luke and shook his hand for Luke to forget it.

"Okay," Luke whispered and hurried back into the crowd. He walked to the front of the basement where there was now standing room only.

"Thank you, Mayor." I bent over and spoke into the microphone. The door opened, and what was left of the day's sun fluttered in, making the figure walking in shadowy. I squinted in hopes it was Dickie Dee so I could arrest him right now on the spot. "Thank you, Luke and Vita, for allowing us this space to come together as a community to discuss not only how amazing Cottonwood is, but to also be updated on the current crime spree."

The door completely closed, and the figure stepped inside.

It was Finn.

Our eyes caught. The edges of his lips ticked up, as did my heart. I gave him a slow blink like Cosmo gave him to let him know how grateful I was for being here to support me.

"What are you going to do about this rash of murders?" someone blurted out.

"I understand y'all are very concerned." I had learned at the academy how to deal with the public by making sure they felt as if everything was about them. "Deputy Lee and I have some promising leads. He's not here because he's following up on one now."

I shot a look at Jasmine and her father. Neither looked impressed.

"What are you going to do about my clients?" Janice stood up. She crossed her arms on her chest. "Not only have you single-handedly ruined their reception as well as their honeymoon, Mrs. Dee needs to have some counseling due to the PTSD the sheriff's department has caused."

"Where is Mr. Dee?" I asked. "If we are going to discuss this here, I would like to know where Mr. Dee is located, because we need to talk to him."

It wasn't the right place for this type of chatter if I were in a big city, but around these parts, we needed every citizen on alert.

Jasmine's face dropped. She blurted out a cry before her father wrapped his arms around her, cradling his little girl to him.

"I'm sorry, Sheriff, but this is not the time and place to discuss the whereabouts of my client. But this is the time to let the good citizens of Cottonwood know we intend to sue the town and you for the damages caused to my clients." Janice was going to go in for the kill.

The chatter was above a whisper as the news fluttered over the room.

Janice was giving a little pause to let the effect of her speech settle in, giving me a glimpse of what was to come if she got me in a courtroom.

Jasmine's dad pulled on Janice's shirt. She bent down to let him whisper something in her ear.

She gave him a nod. He took Jasmine by the hand, and they got up. He cuddled her the entire way to the back of the room, where Jasmine yelled out in tears.

"I believe you will see it differently once the murderer is brought to justice," I assured not only the citizens, but Mayor Ryland. I couldn't help but notice Jasmine was on her cell phone in the back of the room next to Finn.

Finn's face was still. Stern. Serious. He gave me a slow blink letting me know he was listening to the conversation Jasmine was having with whoever was on the other end of the phone.

"If you'll just let me say a few words," Mayor Ryland interrupted and took the microphone. "I understand everyone is on edge, and we are too. We have to let the sheriff do her job in order to apprehend the killer, and if that means stopping a wedding reception or even a honeymoon, then so be it. These two men were someone's sons."

I checked out who Mayor Ryland was looking at, thinking he was giving Janice the what, when, and how, but it was Polly. She was rubbing her belly in the subtle Southern way a mama gives the daddy the what-if-it-were-your-baby look.

Then and there, I knew I was going to have to throw Polly Parker Ryland the baby shower.

"Psst, psst." My head jerked to the sound of someone trying to get my attention.

It was Mama.

Viola had made her way over to Mama, and they were looking at Viola's phone. Ruby was holding her phone up in the air with the screen pointed outward, and Mama was jutting her finger at it like she wanted me to see it.

I squinted.

"Car." Mama made the air motions with her hands of driving a car. Then she pointed to her phone. "On the move."

"Bradley's car," Poppa said as the freight fell over on me.

"Excuse me for a minute." I didn't bother giving Mayor Ryland any sort of explanation and darted through the crowd.

Edna called out a question. It didn't even register with me—it was her voice that I recognized.

"Mama, what are you doing?" I asked her when she and Viola followed me and Finn out of the town council meeting.

All four of us stood in Luke's side yard.

"What do you mean?" Mama poked herself in the chest then poked Viola's arm. "Me and Viola are the ones who tracked him, and me and Viola are going to go find him."

"Ouch." Viola groaned, running her hand over the area where Mama kept poking her.

"You tracked someone?" Finn's eyes grew.

"We are going to lose him." Mama took the first step toward the Wagoneer.

"Mama, you cannot go. This is official business." I held out my hand for Viola's phone. "I need the phone, Viola."

"Give her the phone." Finn didn't mince words. They were stern and hard.

"Fine." Viola slapped her phone on the palm of my hand. "1-2-3-4 is my code to unlock the phone."

The basement door opened.

"Where do you think you're going?" Mayor Ryland stood there, pointing back to the door. "You've got a whole lot of explaining to do to people in there. You've got to give them something. I've stuck my neck out for you tonight."

"You didn't stick your neck out for me," I told him. "You did this for your wife. But I can't stand here because I've got a very important lead."

"Yeah. One me and Viola came up with." Mama's voice had something I'd never heard her have since I was sheriff.

Pride.

"Come on, Kenni!" Poppa hollered from the Wagoneer.

"If you'll excuse me." I took off.

"Kenni, wait!" Finn ran behind me. "You can't just follow a car when you know the owner has been killed. I will come along."

"No." I stopped shy of the Jeep. "You make sure Mama leaves and let me do my job. You don't work here. Remember?"

"I don't like you going after a car when we don't know who is driving."

"I don't have time to tell you everything I found out today, but I have reason, good reason, to believe it's Dickie Dee, since he led me on a car chase." The words fell on Finn. There was a fright in his eyes, telling me he knew he couldn't go with me, but the idea of me, his girlfriend, going alone scared the hell out of him.

"I'll be fine." I gave him a kiss on the cheek and turned to get into the Jeep.

"Kenni, I overheard Jasmine talking to him on the phone. She was begging him to meet her at her parents'. She said something about how her dad would let him do what he wanted for the business and they would work all of this out. She forgives him for the affair." He crossed his arms. "I'm guessing you know all about this?"

"Yes. And now I have to go track a killer." I wagged Viola's phone in the air and jumped in the Jeep.

CHAPTER TWENTY-ONE

The tracker app on Viola's phone was similar to the map app on my phone I used for directions. The little car icon moved as Dickie drove it.

There was no way I was going to use the siren. He'd gotten away from me once. It was not going to happen again.

Everything had to go as smoothly as possible. The car appeared to have stopped in the downtown area, and the closer I drove toward the spot on the map, I realized he'd gone to the inn.

Slowly I passed the car parked exactly where the tracker app reported. No one was in the car, and it was in front of where the wedding party was staying.

"What's going on up in that head of yours?" Poppa asked.

"It would make sense for Dickie to dump his car, since he knows I'm looking for it. And it would be easy for him to have gotten Bradley's keys when he killed Bradley."

"Which would explain why we couldn't find the keys." Poppa snapped his thick fingers. "Now you're thinkin'."

"Jasmine and Dickie didn't go on their honeymoon because he's been hiding out. So from what Finn reported about what she said, it's clear there's something going on that Jasmine is trying to figure out.

Plus she knew about the affair." I drove the Jeep a few more feet before I parked in a vacant spot with Bradley's car in sight from my rearview mirror.

"I say you get on in there and confront him before you have to do something on the street." Poppa was revising our plan.

I got out of the Jeep and pushed the button on the walkie-talkie to Betty Murphy at dispatch.

"Go ahead," Betty answered.

"Betty, it's Kenni." I didn't give her any time to greet me. I kept the button pushed down. "I need you to get Deputy Lee down to the Tattered Covered Books and Inn. I want him to be waiting at the back of the building. I found Dickie Dee driving Bradley's car, and I've got him in the inn. I'm not sure if he'll make a run for it, but I want to make sure Scott is out back if he does."

"Got it." Betty clicked off.

My utility belt rattled as I hurried up the sidewalk toward the car. I kept the palm of my hand on the handle of the gun, with my trigger finger on the holster snap. It would be a quick flick of the finger if I needed to arm myself.

With my back to the car, I stood at the door and glanced inside. Poppa had ghosted into the back seat and looked around.

"Kenni bug, there's a manila envelope back here," Poppa pointed out.

"I need to see if that's the photos of Dickie and the blackmailing." I just named it what it was and not how Brenda Futch had gently put the scheme they were dealing Dickie Dee.

With one eye on the door of the inn, I slowly took my hand off the gun and reached to the door handle, only to find the car was locked.

"And here we go." Poppa somehow used his ghostly self to unlock the door.

"I love having you here." I smiled and reached into the back seat to grab the large envelope.

I peeled back the flap and took out the stack of photos that were not very becoming of a man about to get married.

Instead of taking them with me as evidence since I didn't have the warrant I needed to break into the car, I pulled my phone out to snap some shots. I didn't have anything but circumstantial evidence to arrest Dickie on for murder, but I could certainly take him in for questioning and then get the warrant for not only the cars, but his room.

"Everything has to be done by the book," I told Poppa. "You and I both know Janice will be looking for any loopholes, and we can't have that."

I opened my camera app, and as soon as I did, the pictures I'd gotten off Polly's phone opened automatically.

There were two of Mama talking to Jasmine. Normally I wouldn't even think of it as different, but in one of them Jasmine was a foot taller than Mama.

"This is odd." I used my fingers to blow up the photo and noticed Jasmine had heels on in the taller photo. I swiped to the next photo and noticed she was shorter and the heels were replaced by tennis shoes.

"And look there." Poppa was looking at the picture. "The hem of her dress looks stained."

"Stained," I whispered. "We've got the wrong killer."

"Jasmine Dee." Poppa and I both knew at that instant Jasmine Dee was the killer.

I took a few quick snapshots of the photos of her husband with Brenda's employee before I darted into the inn.

"My stars, Kenni." Nadine jerked up from the front desk when I bolted past her.

"Jasmine Dee?" I stood at the bottom of the steps leading up to the second floor and pointed up.

"Yes." She nodded with big eyes. "She hurried past a few minutes ago, saying they were checking out."

"She might be checking out of here, but she'll be checking into the Cottonwood Sheriff's Department cell." Poppa snickered in delight.

"Dickie?" I asked.

"I've not seen him." She kept her eyes on my gun.

"Do not let anyone leave this inn. Lock the door," I instructed her and flipped the snap off my gun, slowly walking out of the inn so I could hurry to the alley where the steps leading up to the honeymoon suite were located.

Luckily I didn't encounter anyone along the way and felt somewhat better once I climbed the steps and noticed the door to the suite was cracked open. I glanced into the room before I made the decision to wait her out.

"You have made a mess of things." I jerked back and put my back against the outside of the door so I could listen in after I heard Jasmine.

From the sound of things, she was opening drawers and zipping up what sounded like a suitcase, as if she were packing.

"I should've stayed with Bradley Ines when I had the chance. But no, I had to trust you would be the one to take over Daddy's business. And then you go and get caught cheating on me with a hooker? One that you ended up having an affair with? Which was fine until they blackmailed you." Jasmine's footsteps moved away from the door as her voice carried from another room. "Do you think I was just going to let you ruin everything I have worked for? Being Daddy's little girl so I could have the money the company would bring us as soon as I got married and sold it?" A bitter and hard voice poured out of her.

She busted out in a cold laughter.

"Good job at screwing this up. Bradley told me a long time ago how you had a habit of sleeping around. That would've been fine as long as we weren't getting blackmailed." The more she talked, the more I waited. I knew I needed to hear her admit to at least one death.

I curled a shoulder back around the door and twisted my head just enough to see with my eye what was going on.

Jasmine had the suitcase on the floor and was too busy throwing stuff in to have even noticed me or the fact she'd not closed the door all the way. Her back was to the door, so I slid over a little more to get a bigger picture of the room, and that's when I saw Dickie tied up to a chair, with his mouth stuffed with something and her garter belt from the wedding holding it in place around his head.

Dickie's eyes grew big when he saw my shadow cast from the crack. He slid them up to meet mine. I put my finger up to my mouth for him not to say something.

Did he listen to me? No.

Dickie jerked his untied legs, making the chair legs jump up and in the air a few times.

"Now what do you want?" Jasmine asked him through her gritted teeth.

Dickie mumbled through his stuffed mouth and wiggled his head. Jasmine let go of a long sigh and threw the hairdryer on the floor next to the suitcase before she darted over to him and jerked the stuffing out of his mouth.

I moved back around the door and held my gun in position for when Dickie spilled the beans about me being out there.

"I have to go to the bathroom," he said. I closed my eyes as relief settled into my shoulders after he kept me a secret.

"He's going to help you," Poppa had ghosted into the room.

"Fine." Jasmine walked over and grabbed her umbrella from the wedding. "You make any funny moves, and I'll knock you upside your head."

Though I would've loved that to be some sort of admission as to what she'd done with the other umbrella to Gary, it wasn't enough.

Dickie shot me a look, thinking it was enough for me to bolt in and save him. I shook my head and mouthed *more,* rolling my wrist in gesture.

"I agreed to marry you, and after I get the company, to turn it over to you." Dickie started to plead with her. "Please, Jasmine. Let me have this. Let me go, and let me be with Vicky. You don't even love me. You just want the company."

Jasmine jerked on the knots around his wrist as she stood behind the chair, listening to Dickie plead for his freedom.

"You're right, but now that I have to go on the run due to your affair, you should suffer with me." There wasn't a confession from her.

"You don't have to run." Dickie rolled his wrists in circles after they were free. He got up and turned to face her. She shoved the umbrella point in his side.

"You're right." She jabbed him toward the bathroom. "You do. I just gave that sheriff's boyfriend a little show of my own at the town council meeting. Thankfully, you told me about running from her this afternoon. She'd mentioned they had a lead on the killer, and well, I'm so smart I knew it had to be you." She pouted and rubbed her eyes like a baby. "I pretended to cry, boo-hoo, in the meeting, and Daddy took me out. I made it a point to pretend to have gotten a call from you that clearly made you the killer."

"Why? Why didn't we just stick with the plan?" he questioned. "Me and you get married. I take the company. I give you the company, and we get divorced."

"Don't you get it?" she scoffed. "Wait. I thought you had to go to the bathroom. Why all the questions?"

"I just want to know, are you going to kill me like you did Gary and Bradley?" Here was the answer I needed to hear.

"I want you to suffer just like you've made me suffer." She snarled. "Do you think I took pleasure in killing Gary because he was blackmailing you? Then Bradley because he knew?"

"So what's next? Are you going to kill everyone who knows?" he asked, catching her off guard.

"I've had enough of you!" she screamed. She lifted her arm in the air to give him a good whack with the umbrella just as I raised my leg and kicked the door as hard as I could, sending splintered pieces of wood across the room.

"Hold it right there!" I yelled with my gun pointed right at her head. "Put down the umbrella now!"

Jasmine's eyes rounded in shock.

"Clearly she wasn't privy to what an awesome sheriff Kenni Lowry is." Poppa stood next to them, smiling.

"Jasmine Dee, you are under arrest for the murder of Gary Futch." I took a step closer to her as she dropped the umbrella on the floor. With one hand on my gun and the other snapping my cuffs off my utility belt and my eyes on her, I said, "And the murder of Bradley Ines, along with whatever other charges I can get to make sure you never see the light of day again."

CHAPTER TWENTY-TWO

Mama had insisted on throwing a little party for me at Luke and Vita Joneses' movie theater since me, Tibbie Bell, and Jolee Fischer loved to have a girls' movie night. This month's movie was *My Best Friend's Wedding,* and though we'd seen it a million times together already, we knew it would still be fun to watch it again. Only this time Mama wanted all the euchre ladies there too.

Even Polly Parker Ryland had showed up, looking even bigger than she had last week when I saw her at the town council meeting.

It was great to see every one of my friends enjoying a night to celebrate. It'd been a long week, getting Jasmine Dee transported to the state penitentiary, not to even mention the lengthy meetings with Janice Gallo. She knew she didn't stand a chance to win the lawsuit with a killer's motives leading her case. Jasmine's father had also walked away, still in charge of his company. Though Dickie Dee couldn't be charged with anything that would stick, I knew he was going to go straight to Vicky, the woman he'd met through the escort service.

I'd also gone to pay Brenda a visit to let her know I was watching her and her escort business. It was what Poppa had done years ago. When and if I found out there was some sort of illegal gig going on, I'd be at her door quicker than a jackrabbit.

"I'll take another one," I told Vita. My mouth watered just watching her scoop the buttery goodness into a bag. "Thank you."

The popcorn smelled so good and so fresh. I would be back to get another one before the movie started, along with some chocolaty candies to sprinkle down into the bag.

"No, thank you for keeping us safe." Vita handed the bags of warm popcorn to me.

"Just doing my job." I smiled and did that awful thing where I ate a piece of popcorn right off the top of the bag using my mouth instead of my fingers.

"We will all remember that come time for reelection too." Vita winked and moved on to help Viola.

I walked over to Polly and held out one of the bags of popcorn.

"I want to thank you for what you did last week with your husband. You know, getting him on my side at the town council meeting." I wanted to make sure to give credit where credit was due.

"It was the right thing, you know." She batted those big eyes and picked up some of the kernels, tossing them into her mouth. "I told him that I wanted to continue to be the first lady and he needed to support his sheriff."

"That's not a bad idea, to have the same ticket for the election." I did like the idea.

"I told him when he was sitting at the table, gobbling up a pot roast, potatoes, and carrots I'd spent all day in the kitchen preparing. Laundry was piled high on the laundry room floor and bills were stacked on the kitchen counter." Polly painted a not-so-rosy picture of married life. "If he thinks he's going to retire and not afford me the benefits of getting out of that house as the first lady and all the duties that come along with that, he's got another thing coming to him." She rubbed her ever-growing baby belly. "I'm going to get me a nanny, a housekeeper, and a cook when this stinker comes."

Suddenly she gasped.

"What?" I looked down at her stomach and then up to her eyes. "Is the baby okay? You aren't going into labor, are you? Do we need to get you to the hospital? I can put my siren on." The words rushed out of my mouth.

Polly looked up at me and blinked several times. Her mouth was wide open. She pointed behind me.

Oh Lord, was Mama right? Was there going to be a fall wedding? I looked down at Finn Vincent and suddenly my future passed before my eyes.

"Well? I'm waiting." Finn broke into my thoughts.

Though I appeared to be looking down at him while he was on one knee, I was just seeing through him.

Everyone I knew and loved was standing behind Finn, all of them waiting for my answer.

"I know it's not your grandmother's ring. We couldn't find it, but we will continue to look." He held the box even higher. "Kendrick Lowry," he nervously asked, "will you marry me?"

I blinked a few times, recalling how this was exactly what I'd thought I wanted. I certainly didn't want the scenario playing in my head.

I gulped.

"Kenni, um, everyone is waiting on your answer." Finn smiled. His lips quivered on the edges just enough for me to notice the nervousness from me not answering. "I'm kinda feeling like a fool," he said ventriloquist style. "I thought this was what we've been heading toward."

I put a fake smile on my face and looked up behind him where everyone was also waiting. I grazed their heads and noticed Poppa had appeared.

He had his arms folded across his chest. He wasn't as vibrant as when we had a case, and I knew this was the moment.

How was I ever going to choose between the two? A life with Finn by my side in the living? Or the man I respected most in the world in ghost form?

"Kenni?" Finn asked again.

I stood there, not sure what my answer was going to be.

-Will Kenni say yes to Finn? What is going to happen next in Cottonwood?

THE END

If you enjoyed reading this book as much as I enjoyed writing it then be sure to return to the Amazon page and leave a review.

Go to Tonyakappes.com for a full reading order of my novels and while there join my newsletter. You can also find links to Facebook, Instagram and Goodreads.

Well, kiss my grits and call me shocked! Sheriff Kenni Lowry is back to solve a bribery case that's got the town saying Heaven's to Bribery! Continue scrolling for a sneak peek of chapter one.

Chapter One of Book Nine
Heavens To Bribery

Mama always used to say that a woman's life was a series of surprises, but nothing had prepared me for this.

Here I was, the sheriff of Cottonwood, Kentucky, with a murder case half solved, and a man was kneeling before me, proposing in front of my whole family, a couple of townsfolk who'd been drawn by the commotion, and Edna Easterly, the one and only employee of the *Cottonwood Chronicles*. I was sure Mama had hired her for such an occasion as this.

After all, Mama wanted everything on film, and the camera stuck up in my face was certainly going to capture it all.

And I mean all. Including the look on my face.

Finn Vincent, my handsome boyfriend, was looking up at me, his brown eyes filled with hope. I'd seen that look in the eyes of people I'd helped before, but it was never directed at me in this way.

A deafening silence surrounded us, as though all the air had been sucked out of the summer evening. A few steps away, my spectral poppa, the ghost of the former town sheriff in our small town of Cottonwood, Kentucky, had shown up. Only I could see him.

I was on the precipice of answering, my eyes flitting between Finn's hopeful brown gaze and Poppa's ethereal, patient presence. I could feel the weight of Finn's anticipation, a current of electricity humming between us. Poppa, in contrast, emanated calm, a steady beacon in the chaos of this moment.

His phantasmal shoulders lifted in a noncommittal shrug. This decision, he seemed to say, was entirely mine. Thoughts of the murder case that remained unresolved gnawed at my mind, a persistent reminder of my duties as Cottonwood's sheriff, but also the wild unpredictability that life here presented.

"Kenni," Finn whispered, his eyes darting to the left and the right.

His chest filled with air before he looked back up at me, waiting for my answer.

"I..." I began, the word an unfinished symphony hanging in the warm summer air. Finn's gaze was locked on mine, but his attention wavered as my eyes darted past his shoulder in a brief, bewildered glance toward the place where Poppa stood. Of course, Finn could see nothing but empty space.

Abruptly, a scream pierced the quiet evening, like the piercing whistle of a tea kettle reaching the boiling point.

The hair on the back of my neck stood on end, and everyone's focus shifted in unison towards the alarming sound. It was a harsh intrusion, a reminder that stark danger often punctuated Cottonwood's tranquility.

Without a second thought, I found myself moving, an almost automatic reaction, reaching for the trusty weapon holstered around my ankle.

Finn, always quick on his feet, was right behind me. His unanswered proposal hung between us, another silent specter adding to the charged atmosphere.

"Oh Lord!" Mama's voice drifted to us from behind, her tone a cocktail of exasperation and concern. "Can't a woman get proposed to in peace in this town anymore?"

Adrenaline coursed through my veins as we ran out of the makeshift basement movie theater and rounded the corner, heading toward the screaming.

My heart pounded against my ribs like a wild drum. An unexpected sense of relief washed over me—the crisis had provided me a momentary reprieve from answering Finn. But that relief quickly gave way to a sense of dread, a familiar taste of anxiety on my tongue as I imagined the sight we were about to encounter.

In the larger scheme of my life, I knew this incident was merely the start of a new chapter. Another twist in the winding tale of love, duty, and death that defined my existence in Cottonwood. And Finn's proposal, as yet unanswered, would undoubtedly change everything forever.

The frantic cries for help were now louder, echoing through the still night. The voice was unmistakably Patty Dunaway's.

"There!" A long, thin shadow in the moonlight pointed toward the railroad tracks.

Those tracks ran like a metallic scar through the heart of the town, right behind Luke and Vita Jones's house. The stark light of the full moon painted Patty's lanky silhouette against the inky night, forming a tableau of fear and urgency.

Three dog leashes were wrapped around one of her hands as she tried to reel in the dogs attached to them.

With the echoes of Patty's panicked cries still ringing in my ears, I turned to Finn, my voice carrying the firm authority I'd honed as Cottonwood's sheriff. My sheriff mode was like a switch that automatically flipped on and off.

It was completely off when Finn was on one knee, but now that I was standing here with a body lying across the train tracks, the sheriff switch had flipped.

"Finn, I need you to get Patty and the dogs back. And keep the crowd at a distance," I said, motioning to the gathering knot of curious townsfolk who'd begun to drift over from Luke and Vita's.

Although he was no longer part of my department, Finn was someone I trusted implicitly, especially in situations like these. His broad shoulders tensed in understanding, and he nodded, his dark eyes lingering on me for a moment as if he was trying to process how he went from one knee to standing over a body in seconds. He turned toward Patty.

In the soft moonlight, Patty looked even more disheveled than usual. Her frizzy hair was a wild halo around her head, her usually cheerful face pale and stricken with terror. The three dogs she had been walking—a spirited spaniel, a large brindled mutt, and a tiny terrier—whimpered and tugged at their leashes, their sensitive noses detecting that something was wrong.

Finn gently but firmly guided Patty and the canines away from the railway tracks, his calming presence seeming to soothe them slightly.

Meanwhile, the inquisitive onlookers who'd followed us from the movie theater were held at bay by Finn's commanding stature, their speculative whispers and concerned glances creating a subdued background buzz.

From the edges of the curious crowd, Mama's voice rang out. Her distinctive southern twang was a comforting soundtrack to most of my life, but right now it rang through the night with an edge of anxiety.

"Finn Vincent, what in heaven's name is going on?" Mama demanded. Her slightly accusatory tone betrayed her concern, an emotion she was quick to share. "Don't y'all worry. Kenni will get to the bottom of this, and we will be back to Finn's proposal in no time."

Finn looked flustered, glancing back at me before turning to Mama. "Kenni is doing her job. We should let her—"

"There's someone on the tracks," Patty said in a shaky voice.

"But I didn't hear no train, did y'all?" Mama cut him off, turning to her companions with a challenging look on her face.

Her question was aimed at her small posse of friends, three formidable ladies who were among the most influential business owners in Cottonwood.

Viola White, the owner of White's Jewelry, was a petite woman who stood just five feet, four inches. Her gray hair was styled immaculately.

Beside her, Ruby Smith, the owner of Ruby's Antiques, was a stark contrast. Her short red hair was as fiery as her personality, and her vibrant orange lipstick only added to her overall vivid personality.

Then there was Lulu McClain, who owned Lulu's Boutique. Her very short black hair and pronounced southern accent made her a distinctive character. She had a motherly quality that put people at ease and a sense of style that made her boutique the talk of the town.

With the crowd momentarily placated, I turned my attention back to the body. My heart pounded in my chest as I crouched down beside the figure, and the sharp smell of iron filled my nostrils. I fumbled for my phone and turned the screen's brightness up to its maximum, providing the only other source of illumination against the moonlit darkness.

Holding my breath, I pointed the flashlight toward the body, preparing myself for what was to come next. Regardless of who the victim was, this night was clearly taking a turn that none of us had expected.

Though I was all too familiar with this part of my job, the sight of a life so brutally snuffed out still caused my stomach to twist uneasily. Yet I couldn't let emotion sway me. I had a crime scene to survey, a growing crowd to manage, and a murder to solve.

"Who is it, Kenni?" Mama's voice cut through the silent night, her curiosity echoing in the hushed crowd. As I hesitated, she added, more to her friends than me, "Kenni will tell us."

Her confidence in me was comforting, but in this moment, it felt misplaced. I had no answer to give her, no name to assign to the lifeless body before me. Despite the shock of the situation, I was surprisingly calm, my mind beginning to fall into the familiar rhythm of deductive reasoning.

The man was a stranger to me, a face I had never seen in the tightly knit community of Cottonwood. His dark hair was matted with blood, and his clothes were nondescript, the kind that wouldn't draw attention in any crowd. I felt a pang of sadness at the sight of a life extinguished under the cover of darkness, far from home.

Mama had been right about something, though. There hadn't been a train. Cottonwood was a town molded by routine and rhythm, and the chugging of the trains passing through was as regular as the sunrise. A long, drawn-out whistle usually announced their arrival, breaking the silence of the night with a mechanical howl that could be heard all the way to the Jones's basement. The sound had woven itself into the fabric of our lives, an auditory reminder of the outside world.

There was no such sound tonight. No whistle, no rumbling of wheels against the tracks, no rhythmic clacking of the cargo. The silence was a stark contradiction to the chaotic scene that had unfolded. And it wasn't just the silence. Looking more closely, I could see the lack of typical gruesome injuries that one would associate with a train accident.

The moonlight glinted off the rails, unblemished and smooth. There was no sign that a train had rushed over this body. My gut twisted with unease as the implications of my observations sank in. This was not an accident. This was something much darker.

I slowly stood up, tucking away my phone and turning to face the anxious crowd.

"I need everyone to stay back," I said, trying to keep my voice steady. "This is a crime scene. We need to preserve it until help arrives. So why don't you all go on home, and we will have some details in the morning. We won't have anything here tonight."

I locked eyes with Finn, giving him a curt nod. He understood, moving quickly to usher Patty and her dogs away from the tracks and back toward the crowd. As a murmur of confusion and fear rippled through the townsfolk, I took a deep breath, preparing myself for the tumultuous investigation that lay ahead. This night was far from over.

Heavens To Bribery is now available to purchase.!

BOOKS BY TONYA
SOUTHERN HOSPITALITY WITH A SMIDGEN OF HOMICIDE

Camper & Criminals Cozy Mystery Series

All is good in the camper-hood until a dead body shows up in the woods.

BEACHES, BUNGALOWS, AND BURGLARIES
DESERTS, DRIVING, & DERELICTS
FORESTS, FISHING, & FORGERY
CHRISTMAS, CRIMINALS, AND CAMPERS
MOTORHOMES, MAPS, & MURDER
CANYONS, CARAVANS, & CADAVERS
HITCHES, HIDEOUTS, & HOMICIDES
ASSAILANTS, ASPHALT & ALIBIS
VALLEYS, VEHICLES & VICTIMS
SUNSETS, SABBATICAL AND SCANDAL
TENTS, TRAILS AND TURMOIL
KICKBACKS, KAYAKS, AND KIDNAPPING
GEAR, GRILLS & GUNS
EGGNOG, EXTORTION, AND EVERGREEN
ROPES, RIDDLES, & ROBBERIES
PADDLERS, PROMISES & POISON
INSECTS, IVY, & INVESTIGATIONS
OUTDOORS, OARS, & OATH
WILDLIFE, WARRANTS, & WEAPONS
BLOSSOMS, BBQ, & BLACKMAIL
LANTERNS, LAKES, & LARCENY
JACKETS, JACK-O-LANTERN, & JUSTICE
SANTA, SUNRISES, & SUSPICIONS
VISTAS, VICES, & VALENTINES
ADVENTURE, ABDUCTION, & ARREST
RANGERS, RVS, & REVENGE

Killer Coffee Cozy Mystery Series

Welcome to the Bean Hive Coffee Shop where the gossip is just as hot as the coffee.

Holiday Cozy Mystery Series

CELEBRATE GOOD CRIMES!

FOUR LEAF FELONY
MOTHER'S DAY MURDER
A HALLOWEEN HOMICIDE
NEW YEAR NUISANCE
CHOCOLATE BUNNY BETRAYAL
FOURTH OF JULY FORGERY
SANTA CLAUSE SURPRISE
APRIL FOOL'S ALIBI

Kenni Lowry Mystery Series

Mysteries so delicious it'll make your mouth water and leave you hankerin' for more.

FIXIN' TO DIE
SOUTHERN FRIED
AX TO GRIND
SIX FEET UNDER
DEAD AS A DOORNAIL
TANGLED UP IN TINSEL
DIGGIN' UP DIRT
BLOWIN' UP A MURDER
HEAVENS TO BRIBERY

Magical Cures Mystery Series

Welcome to Whispering Falls where magic and mystery collide.

A CHARMING CRIME
A CHARMING CURE
A CHARMING POTION (novella)
A CHARMING WISH

A CHARMING SPELL
A CHARMING MAGIC
A CHARMING SECRET
A CHARMING CHRISTMAS (novella)
A CHARMING FATALITY
A CHARMING DEATH (novella)
A CHARMING GHOST
A CHARMING HEX
A CHARMING VOODOO
A CHARMING CORPSE
A CHARMING MISFORTUNE
A CHARMING BLEND (CROSSOVER WITH A KILLER COFFEE COZY)
A CHARMING DECEPTION

Mail Carrier Cozy Mystery Series

Welcome to Sugar Creek Gap where more than the mail is being delivered.

STAMPED OUT
ADDRESS FOR MURDER
ALL SHE WROTE
RETURN TO SENDER
FIRST CLASS KILLER
POST MORTEM
DEADLY DELIVERY
RED LETTER SLAY

About Tonya

Tonya has written over 100 novels, all of which have graced numerous bestseller lists, including the USA Today. *Best known for stories charged with emotion and humor and filled with flawed characters, her novels have garnered reader praise and glowing critical reviews. She lives with her husband and a very spoiled rescue cat named Ro. Tonya grew up in the small southern Kentucky town of Nicholasville. Now that her four boys are grown men, Tonya writes full-time in her camper she calls her SHAMPER (she-camper).*

Learn more about her be sure to check out her website tonyakappes.com. Find her on Facebook, Twitter, BookBub, and Instagram

Sign up to receive her newsletter, where you'll get free books, exclusive bonus content, and news of her releases and sales.

If you liked this book, please take a few minutes to leave a review now! Authors (Tonya included) really appreciate this, and it helps draw more readers to books they might like. Thanks!

Cover artist: Mariah Sinclair: The Cover Vault

www.ingramcontent.com/pod-product-compliance
Ingram Content Group UK Ltd.
Pitfield, Milton Keynes, MK11 3LW, UK
UKHW021650190726
13853UKWH00001B/180

9 798830 355537